THEIR MARCHIONESS

THEIRS
BOOK ONE

JESS MICHAELS

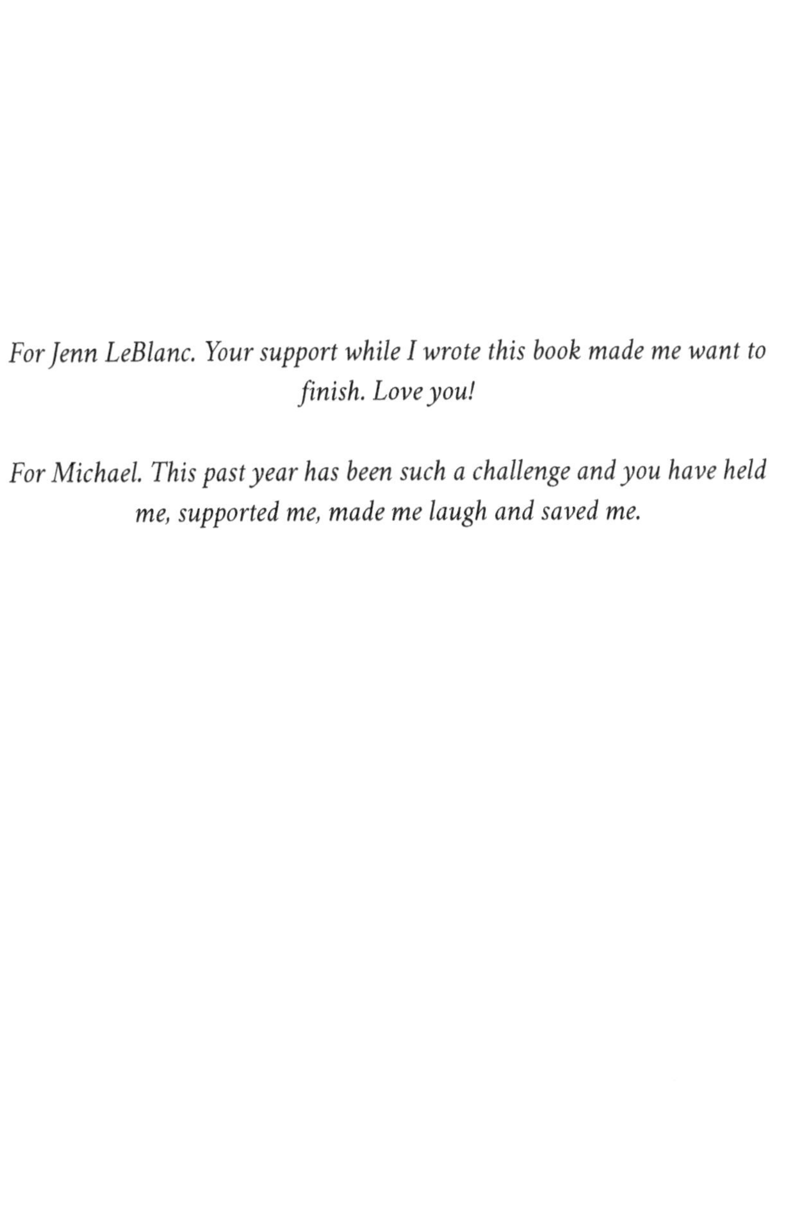

For Jenn LeBlanc. Your support while I wrote this book made me want to finish. Love you!

For Michael. This past year has been such a challenge and you have held me, supported me, made me laugh and saved me.

CHAPTER 1

Elliot

The Marquess of Egerton, had wanted his wife, Merritt, from the first moment he saw her, over a decade before. Elliot had, of course, not been the only one. With her sleek red hair, her bright blue-green eyes and her outrageously kissable lips, she had been one of the most sought-after debutantes of her coming out year. A true Diamond of the First Water. And yet she'd always seemed disinterested in the popinjays who bobbed around her, trying to gain her attention.

So Elliot had gone about the delicate business of winning her. It had been a two-pronged plan, the first of which was convincing his own father that a marriage contract was his idea. The late marquess had never done anything that wasn't in his best interest.

The second had been making Merritt notice him. That one had been trickier. Complimenting her beauty had resulted in yawns, so he had pursued her beyond her looks, and found the layers of her mind and her soul were even more attractive than the lush package they were wrapped in.

Both parts of his plan had ultimately succeeded, and so today, over ten years into their union, he found himself looking across the carriage from her. She was as beautiful now as she had been the moment they were wed. More beautiful, actually. She had come into her own as marchioness. Grown into her sophistication in her hair and dress, and her eyes, those amazing eyes he couldn't stop staring into, held even more knowledge and sensuality.

She smiled and glanced up from her book. "Going to keep staring all day, Egerton?"

He arched a brow and tried to suppress his own smile. "I will stare all I want, my lady."

Her expression went from something playful to something more focused, erotic, and she set the book aside entirely. "Are you going to ever tell me exactly where we are going and what we are doing?"

He shrugged one shoulder. "What would be the fun if you knew all my secrets?"

There was a moment when something just a touched pained crossed her face, but she erased it swiftly enough. Still, he had seen it. He understood it. As much as they were connected, respected each other, desired each other, even after all this time it was still difficult for him to give all of himself. He wanted to, but there was always something keeping him back. Several somethings, actually.

So he gave what he could and hoped it would be enough.

"You think I could not deduce at least a fraction of the truth?" she asked.

He tilted his head. "I'm sure given enough time you might even be able to deduce all of it. You are, after all, the most intelligent person I have ever known."

Her eyes brightened with pleasure at that compliment, still her favorite of anything he ever noted about her when he waxed poetic. Still the truest of all the pretty words that ever fell from his lips while he dragged them over her body.

"Let me see…I know it has something to do with my birthday," she began, ticking off one finger with the other. "That isn't much of a secret."

"Turning thirty is not something to be ignored," Elliot conceded. "But as you said, nothing of a secret to that."

"But you did not wish to have the children present for it, nor any other friends or family," she continued, and licked her lips. Just to tease him, he thought. "So I have a feeling this private celebration is something very…intimate."

"Very intimate," he agreed, and found his throat thick with desire.

She smiled again. "Good. You have been so busy the last few months, you and I have hardly had any real time together to…" She hesitated and leaned forward. "To play. And I've missed that."

He caught her hand and drew it to his lips, dragging them over her palm, her wrist. Until her breath hitched. She wasn't wrong. Oh, they'd made love plenty of times during the last few months. He never went more than a day or maybe two without having her. But they'd done nothing special. They hadn't gone to the Donville Masquerade together, as was their habit, or set aside a whole day or even a few days to make a thorough exploration of each other.

The carriage began to slow, so there was no time to do a little preview of what was to come right here and now. He released her hand and motioned to the window. "We are arriving now, so your suspense will soon be allayed."

She pulled the curtain aside and together they peered out. The cottage was not huge, but it was finely situated, perched on a bluff that overlooked the sea, with a path leading down to the beach beyond.

"Oh, Elliot," she breathed. "How lovely!"

"And all ours for a week," he said, knowing he was leaving out some details, but she would find them out soon enough. "The servants will make all the final preparations and then go into Brighton for their own holidays. Food will be delivered and the house tidied mid-week, but otherwise we will be blissfully left to our own devices."

She clapped her hands together with real pleasure. "Oh, I'm so glad. This will be wonderful, Elliot. I cannot wait."

The carriage stopped before he could respond, and then the hustle and bustle of arrival began. He helped her from the carriage and sent her off to do her duties, as he did his own, verifying all the timing of comings and goings with the footmen and drivers.

After about half an hour, he entered the cottage. Two maids were uncovering furniture and fluffing decorative pillows in the parlor off the little foyer. He heard another in the kitchen, taking care of the food for the next few days.

He made his way up the stairs and down the hall to the bedroom in the back of the house. He opened the door and heard Merritt in the dressing room with her maid, Cora. They were lightly chatting together, as they often did. He paused a moment to listen to just the sound of her, the rhythm of her voice and laughter. His favorite music.

With a sigh, he went to the doorway and leaned on the frame, watching them until Merritt straightened and looked at him. "Egerton," she said softly.

"My lady," he returned with a slow incline of his head. "I have one thing to take care of before our escape can truly begin, so I must step out. It may take me an hour or so."

Merritt blinked. "Oh. Well, we're almost finished here, so I suppose that will give me a bit of time to myself."

He nodded. "Yes. And I'll hurry back."

She wrinkled her brow, as if she sensed he wasn't being completely honest. Trust her to notice even the tiniest changes that would reveal him. But she didn't address the issue and merely nodded. "Then I'll see you shortly. Be careful."

He inclined his head again and exited the room and down the stairs to leave the house. A horse was waiting for him there, and Elliot smiled, even as his heart throbbed with nervousness.

He had so many plans for Merritt in the next seven days. And once he was gone, the first step in those plans would commence. He only hoped that everything would work out as he hoped. Because if it went wrong, it could well go very wrong, indeed.

Merritt

Merritt moved around the bedchamber she would share with Elliot for the next week and shivered as she placed candles and checked drawers to make sure everything they needed was in its proper place. Cora was still here, of course, but this was not a duty for her, and so she'd sent the maid downstairs to help with whatever the other servants were doing.

What Merritt was readying was private...intimate.

Normally she would only focus on the anticipatory thrill such preparation stirred in her body, but in that moment she was troubled. Elliot had always been difficult to read. In truth, that had been one of the things that drew her to him. While all the other men grasping for her hand and the fortune that went along with it talked and talked and talked, Elliot had often only speared her with that dark gaze.

And made more promises with his eyes than he ever made with his lips. Her attraction to him had been immediate and powerful and...troubling at first, for so many reasons. And yet she hadn't been able to resist him and his relentless drive to have her. Their marriage, though one ostensibly of convenience to start, had transformed rapidly into one of deep passion and true companionship.

She knew him, even with all his secrets. And today he had been keeping something from her. She'd seen it in the dart of his gaze, in the flex of his hand at his side. His little tells, ones she'd observed over the years and memorized.

What were his plans? And why did they feel so...dangerous?

There was a light rap on the partially closed door and she turned to find Cora had returned. "I beg your pardon, my lady, but you've a caller."

Merritt drew back in surprise and confusion. "A—a caller? *Here?*"

"Yes. He's awaiting you in the parlor."

Merritt shook her head and started downstairs, her mind racing. A gentleman caller at that. It could be one of the neighboring gentry, of course, having heard that the marquess and his wife were visiting. She would have to hurry him along so that she would have Elliot to herself when he returned.

"He says he was asked by the marquess, my lady," Cora added as they reached the hall.

Merritt jerked her face toward Cora. "Does he?" she asked. "Well, that is surprising."

Who would Elliot call here as an interruption to their week of sin and pleasure? It made no sense.

She nodded to Cora. "Go ahead and finish with the rest. Unless I ring for you, assume you can depart when you originally planned."

"Leave you alone with a stranger?" Cora asked, blinking.

"Egerton will be back presently," Merritt pointed out. "And I *will* ring if I'm uncomfortable and would like a buffer."

"Yes, my lady," Cora said, and shot her one last concerned look before she moved along.

Merritt smoothed her hands along her gown before she opened the door and stepped in to greet the intruder who had come here. She took three steps into the room and then stopped short to stare at the beautiful man at the mantel. He had blond hair, a hint of scruff on perfectly angled cheeks, bright green eyes and the most beautiful mouth she'd ever seen.

A mouth she had intimate knowledge of, even if it was over a decade before. She fought to find her voice and somehow managed to choke out, "P-Peter."

The color had left his face when she entered the parlor and he moved a long step toward her, closing a bit of the distance that was between them. "Merry," he breathed, then shook his head. "What in the world are you doing here?"

CHAPTER 2

Peter

Merry was here. That was the only cogent thought Peter Reid's addled brain could manage to conjure over and over again as he stared at her. Drank her in with all her stunning and sensual beauty that had been haunting his dreams since the moment they'd been parted, a lifetime ago.

It wasn't that he hadn't known the wife of his patron, the Marquess of Egerton, was Merritt. He just tried not to think about it. About her and her relationship with the other man.

Ever.

"What am *I* doing here?" she repeated, shaking her head. "That is not the question, Peter. What are *you* doing here? And apparently you told my maid that you were called here by Elliot...by my husband. What in the world is going on?"

Peter fought to arrange his spinning mind, to put the pieces together that neither of them could see. "The marquess did call me to meet him here, as he apparently knew I would be in the area on holiday this month. I came because he has been...he's my patron, Merritt."

She blinked, and what he'd always feared was true became clear. She hadn't known that the marquess provided the funding behind Peter's rise as a playwright, his dream come true after years of struggle and strife. Egerton had some other motive behind it rather than her urging.

"Your patron," she repeated, and staggered away to the window, where she stared out at the waves crashing onto the beach below. "He never told me. Even when we spoke of your work."

"You spoke of my work?" Peter asked softly.

She faced him then, her gaze pointed. "Of course. You are the toast of London theatre, Peter. Your name comes up often in our circles. If I refused to discuss you, it would appear...odd to him. Elliot has supported many a thespian, but never behind my back." She moved toward him. "You've met with him then? Spoken to him?"

Peter swallowed hard as he thought of the tall, dark and devastatingly handsome Marquess of Egerton. He'd met the man, yes. Seen him often in many settings. Some of them not particularly savory, at least to the masses. And Egerton *always* approached him. Always held him captive with his dark stare, always made Peter very aware of him, and of her by proxy.

Not that they ever discussed her.

"I have," he admitted.

"Does he know...know..." She trailed off and dropped her gaze to the floor.

"That you and I once cared for each other?"

Now Peter couldn't help but move closer to her. Too close considering they were alone now. He'd heard the servants leaving a moment before. They were alone and he wanted to be near her because he hadn't been for over a decade and his body actually ached for her.

She lifted her blue-green gaze. "Once?"

The way she said that one word, it was like she'd grabbed his still-broken heart and squeezed. He reached for her, dragging his fingers along the bare expanse of her forearm. He shouldn't have, of course, but he couldn't resist.

She still felt like silk.

Peter, she mouthed, rather than say his name out loud.

He curled his fingers around her arm now, drawing her even closer. Her breasts brushed his chest, her breath stirred against his chin as she stared up at him with longing and regret and fear and desire all merged into a potent cocktail.

He was going to kiss her. When he did, it would destroy everything in his world. Perhaps in hers, too. And he hated himself for it even as he lowered his mouth toward hers anyway.

"Good afternoon, Mr. Reid, Merritt."

They froze at the voice at the door and for a heartbeat no one moved. But then Merritt yanked away from him and pivoted to face the marquess, who now stood in the doorway, watching them through a hooded and unreadable gaze.

Elliot

"Elliot!" Merritt gasped, shaking her head as she lifted a trembling hand toward him and then dropped it to her side. "I...we..."

She couldn't think of anything to say, of course. Elliot didn't expect her to, though. He had arranged for this moment, assumed it would happen. He almost regretted it now, seeing the pain and confusion on his wife's beautiful face. She was hurting. She would hurt a little more before this was over.

But then he hoped to make it all worthwhile.

"Elliot," she said, this time a little calmer. "What is going on?"

He arched a brow and motioned toward Peter Reid. He tried not to look at him. Tried not to mark his broad shoulders, the way his harsh jawline was outlined above the wrap of his crisp cravat.

"Your gift, my lady," he said.

"My *gift?*" she repeated, outrage replacing the regret in her tone. "What the bloody hell does that mean?"

He moved to her and she stepped back. Oh, she was angry, his spitfire of a wife. It had been a long time since he'd seen such a spark in her eyes. It excited him, though. Her passion in upset always led to an explosive reunion in the end. He very much looked forward to it.

"Have I not always given you what you wanted, Merritt?" he asked softly, slowly. "Did you think I limited that to objects? This is a very important birthday. Why not give you something…*someone* who has always been out of your reach?"

Her expression twisted and he saw that she was beginning to understand why he'd asked Reid here. What he expected to happen. What he *wanted* to happen, though that part she might not fully grasp yet. That this was a gift for him as much as for her.

"You bastard," she whispered. "How dare you go behind my back? How dare you manipulate a situation that you cannot begin to understand? How dare you?"

She didn't wait for his response, but turned on her heel and stalked from the room. He heard their door slam upstairs a moment later and sighed as he turned to Reid with a shake of his head. "She will come around."

Reid stepped forward. "Come around to what, my lord? What exactly did you demand I come here to do?"

Elliot arched a brow toward him and folded his arms. "Come now, Reid. You and I have known each other for many years and this has been an open secret between us for just as long, yes?"

Peter shifted, a little color entering those astonishing high cheekbones of his. "I don't know what you mean."

Elliot snorted and walked to the sideboard to pour himself a drink. "Did you think I wouldn't find out that you were her first love? The love torn from her by her wretched father? The love that changed her and helped mold her into everything she is today?"

He pivoted and held Peter's stare. "Please don't treat me like a fool."

Once again Peter shifted. "I…I thought you might know, yes. A man like you would know everything."

Arrogant pride filled Elliot at that. "I do try. And at first I will admit that my reaction was one of…well, it wasn't a pretty feeling." He swallowed hard because the memory made him taste the unpleasant tang of jealousy instead of the whisky in his glass. "But the years since my discovery of this truth have softened me. And so here we are."

"Here we are doing what, exactly?" Peter asked.

Elliot took another sip of his drink and then handed it to Peter. The other man hesitated a moment before he took it and finished the drink. Elliot couldn't help but mark that Peter placed his lips exactly where his own had been. He couldn't deny the little flare of hunger that fact caused, too.

And tamped it down because there was no place for it.

"As I said to her before she stormed off to pace around our bedroom in an aroused rage, I want Merritt to have what she desires. Especially for her birthday."

"And that's me," Peter said carefully.

Elliot inclined his head. "I think, in truth, it is *us*."

There was a pause that seemed to last forever before Peter whispered, "Us."

Elliot nodded. "She is not the innocent girl she was when last you were with her. Over the years together, she has honed appetites that I've encouraged. Desires that…" He licked his lips. "Good God, when she gives over to them, it is something to behold."

Peter's breath caught, just a fraction. But enough for Elliot to know that his words were hitting the mark he wanted.

"One of the things she likes to read about, to watch, to fantasize about…is two men with a woman. With that woman being the center of their attention and care. She's never asked for it. We've never indulged in bringing another to our bed. But now seems as good a time as any. And you are the perfect pick since it seems you are business that was left unfinished in her past. And I know you to be a discreet gentleman with a reputation for keeping your lovers…satisfied."

Peter's hand clenched at his side. His pupils were dilated with desire he didn't seem entirely ready to come around to. He nodded toward the door. "A very pretty image to play in my mind, my lord. But your wife doesn't seem as keen on the idea."

"But you are," Elliot asked. "If you had the chance to have her, to share her, you would wish to do so?"

There was a beat, then two, that passed between the question and his answer. "Yes," Peter said softly, at last. "I would very much want that."

"Excellent," Elliot said, relief and desire merging in his blood in that charged moment. "Then leave the rest to me."

Merritt

Merritt couldn't stop shaking as she paced her way around the chamber. Her mind raced with the unbelievable events that had just transpired. Seeing Peter again after all these years apart? Having Elliot be the orchestrator of that reunion? And then her husband wanting her to…to what, exactly? Make love to Peter?

She shivered at that thought. He'd been her first love and yet she'd been so careful never to throw that in Elliot's face. She'd kept the past to herself, the hole Peter had left behind in her heart ignored.

And secretly Elliot had known all along?

As she pivoted yet again, the door to the bedchamber opened and Elliot stepped in. She didn't think or plan, just raced toward him in a few long strides.

"How could you do that?" she burst out, lifting her hands to…

well, she wasn't exactly certain what. Strike him? It was what she wanted to do right now as he looked at her with that impassive expression, like he hadn't just stripped her entire world apart.

He caught her wrists before she could do something so foolhardy, but instead of pushing her away, he yanked her close, all the way against his chest so she could feel him down the entire length of her body.

"Do you think after all these years," he said, using that low, commanding tone he knew drove her mad, "after every time I've played your body like an instrument, that I don't know what you desire, Merritt?"

She'd been fighting him, pulling against him, but now she stopped and just stared up into his face. "Elliot—"

"That I haven't heard your breath catch when you hear someone talk about the plays of Peter Reid?" He leaned in closer, his lips nearly brushing hers. "That I don't know you pore over every article that is written about him, every review?"

He didn't sound angry even though everything he'd just said had to be seen as a betrayal. She felt guilty about it as he spoke, wished she could deny his charges when she couldn't.

She tugged, and this time he released her. She staggered back, struggling to catch her breath in the quiet of the room. She smoothed her hands over her skirts as if she could rub away her tangled emotions.

"How long?" she whispered.

He was silent for a fraction of a moment. "Since my father died. When I was going through his effects, I found letters sent between him and your father. They were written at the beginning of our courtship and after our engagement. Both were worrying over the influence of this lost love of yours. How Peter Reid would impact our union."

She turned her face. Part of her just felt terrible that Elliot had learned the truth in such a horrible way, at the height of what had

been one of the most difficult times of his life. But the other part...
the other part made her seethe all over again.

"Elliot," she said, clenching her hands at her sides. "Your father
died *eight* years ago. You've known about Peter for eight years and
you never said a word to me? You just went behind my back and...
did what? Hunted him?"

His mouth tightened in displeasure. "I supported his career.
Helped him become the celebrated playwright he was meant to be."

"You bastard," she choked out. "Why didn't you just speak
to me?"

He moved toward her again and his expression had softened in
the slightest. "Because, my dear, you are allowed your past. Your
fantasies. I've always accepted them, haven't I? Nurtured them when
I could." He reached out and dragged his fingers along her cheek.
Despite her emotions, she couldn't help but shiver at the electric
awareness his touch always created in her. "How is this any
different?"

He turned her so her back was to him, pulling her against his
chest. She shut her eyes, sensation washing over her, mixing with
the confusion she felt. It was a potent mixture.

"It is entirely different," she said, glancing over her shoulder at
him as he began to unfasten her gown one button after another. It
was so hard to focus when he did that. She had to believe that was
his purpose. "You brought Peter here to...what in the world did you
want him to do? Want *me* to do?"

"What I want is for you to have your pleasure. Your fantasy."

He pushed her gown forward, then over her hips. She stepped
out of the circle of fabric and turned to face him. She knew that
look on his face so well. He wanted her. Not just wanted her,
wanted to utterly devour her. To make her come until she was
weak. She shivered.

"And you think my fantasy is having him?" she asked.

He nodded slowly and looped his fingers beneath her chemise so he could glide it from her body, leaving her naked. "Having him. Having me. Having us."

Her eyes went wide. "You both. Together?"

She said it and her mind went wild with images of just such a thing. They bombarded her with a dozen scenarios that brought her right to the edge of orgasm without either man ever touching her.

And then Elliot did. His fingers slid between her thighs, stroked upward, dragging the tips through the wetness of her sex. He smiled as he lifted them and let her see the shiny evidence.

"Both of us together, Merritt," he agreed. "I will share you for your pleasure. For my own."

He leaned in and his mouth caught hers. She couldn't resist him. She'd never been able to. She wound her arms around his neck, lifting into him, reveling in the push of his tongue through her lips, the grip of his hands as he slid them down her back and cupped her backside. He massaged the curve of her, grinding her against him, and she whimpered into his mouth.

"Should I call him in?" he asked, putting his hand back between her legs. He began to circle her clitoris with his fingers, bringing throbbing, desperate pleasure there. She dipped her head back, trying to maintain purchase and control. Knowing it wasn't possible.

He would take what he wanted. He would give when he wanted. He would have her on her knees, probably quite literally, when he was finished. And she would love every minute of it. And the idea that he would bring Peter into that potent mix? That he would allow her what she had been denied for so many years?

That wasn't something she could deny.

"Yes," she gasped. "Call him."

CHAPTER 3

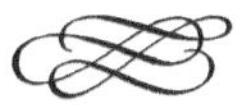

Peter

Peter had been standing in the hall outside the bedchamber for around a quarter of an hour, but it had felt like the longest lifetime. He stared at the shut door, too thick to hear the occupants inside and tried to imagine just what the hell was happening in there.

When the marquess had asked him to meet here, Peter had to admit that a dozen thoughts had gone through his mind. One of them had been that perhaps Egerton, himself, wanted to meet for an assignation. After all, Peter was well aware of the tension in the air between them any time they were together. They exchanged...*looks*. And he was a man with enough experience to know what those looks meant.

But now he had to wonder if that had always been about Merry after all. Sharing Merry.

The idea of it...all of it...made Peter hard as steel. The only reason why he'd at all entertain the notion of fucking Merritt while her husband watched. Or played along.

"Christ," Peter muttered, and ran a hand through his hair.

The door to the chamber opened and Egerton motioned him in. Peter drew a deep breath and entered. He came to a stop just inside and stared at the remarkable vision before him.

Merry was on the huge bed on the opposite side of the room, propped up on pillows. She was entirely naked. He'd never seen her naked and it was…spectacular. His mouth dropped open as he took her in, all gorgeous curves that led to a wet sex between her spread legs. She was practically writhing, like she'd already been set on edge.

He glanced at Egerton and the marquess arched a brow and shrugged ever so slightly. His doing, it seemed. He and Merry had obviously come to an accord.

"Go to her," Egerton said softly. "Touch her."

Peter could barely breathe as he stared at Egerton and then let his gaze slide back to Merry. The marquess's order echoed in his ears, low and hungry. It only added to the erotic element of this situation.

It was also an order Peter found he couldn't deny. He moved to her slowly, staring as he got closer and closer. Her nipples were hard as pebbles, her lips were wet and slightly parted. Her gaze was glassy with desire.

"Peter?" she whispered.

It was a question. A request for permission to want this. And he realized in that moment that he would never deny her. He couldn't. Not after all this time apart, after all the fantasies of just this moment when she was spread out in offering before him.

"May I touch you?" he asked.

She nodded, desperate. "Please!" she cried out.

He glanced back toward the marquess and found Egerton had moved forward, his gaze sharp as he watched them. There was no denying his dilated pupils, nor the outline of his hard cock against his trousers. Egerton was as aroused by this as they both were.

Peter extended a shaking hand and cupped Merry's chin. She

lifted into him, sitting up as he took her mouth like he hadn't been able to do earlier in the sitting room. The kiss was gentle for but a brief moment and then years of denial turned it wild.

She moaned against his lips and he drove into her, hard and harsh and claiming even though she wasn't his. She'd never be his, even if he fucked her for days on end. But she still tasted like honey and mint, and he wanted to make her legs shake with pleasure.

He cupped one breast, squeezing and stroking and pinching the sensitive nipple as she shuddered with pleasure beneath him. He slid his hand lower, across her belly and her hip and her thighs, which she parted even wider.

He pulled away then so he could look at his hand on her skin. Look at his fingers as he drew them to the inside of her thigh and then up to cup her wet, hot sex.

Her shaky, hungry cry was so animal that he nearly spent right there and then. He was so focused on her, on touching her, that he hadn't noticed Egerton had moved. He leaned in closer, his body heat permeating Peter's jacket as he passed by. The marquess climbed onto the bed, dragging a hand up the center of Merry's trembling body and then stroking his thumb across her lip as she licked and bit at him.

Gently, he positioned himself behind her on the pillows, shifting her until she was sprawled against his chest. He met Peter's eyes as he cupped his wife's breasts and began to stroke gently, then harder, strumming her nipples as she turned her face against him with gasps and moans.

"Make her come," Egerton ordered. "With your mouth. Now."

Merritt

Merritt heard Elliot's outrageous order. She almost came undone with just those words. With his touch against her breasts merged with Peter's fingers pressed against her pussy. She stared down at him. Would he do as Elliot asked? Or would this prove to be too much and make him back away?

Peter answered without words. Slowly he pressed his knee into the mattress, joining them on the big bed. He pushed between her legs slowly, moving onto his stomach so that his face was close to her sex. She gasped as he brushed the roughness of his cheek against her inner thigh. And then his tongue moved across her slit in a long, heavy stroke.

It was electric pleasure, almost too intense, and it shot through every nerve ending in her body. She arched and Elliot chuckled behind her, pressing her down and holding her steady for the torturous pleasure.

Peter peeled her open, his thumbs massaging the tender flesh of her outer lips, and returned his mouth to her. He licked her over and over, gentle then hard, stroking every fold, tasting her like she was the sweetest feast. She lifted toward him, riding his tongue, trying to find the flick of it that would send her over the edge.

He didn't allow it, smiling against her as he looked up her body, watching her as he pleasured her.

Above her she felt Elliot shift, felt the hardness of his cock against her back. She pushed back against him, grinding ever so gently, and he rumbled at the movement and pinched her nipples a little harder. She looked up and found him focused not on her, but Peter. His hungry expression was one she knew very well. It was the same way he watched her across a room at a ball, the same way he watched her when she mounted him in their bed or took him into her mouth.

He was watching Peter with *desire,* and that fact made her legs start to shake as her pleasure increased. At the same moment Peter shifted his tongue's attention from teasing to something with more purpose. He tapped it against her clitoris, then he began to suck. Hard and steady, over and over.

She clutched at Elliot's thick thighs, unable to suppress her keening cries of pleasure as she was dragged up to and finally over the cliff of orgasm. She heard the neediness, the wildness to her moans as they echoed in the air around her. She bucked against the waves that seemed never ending, and Peter never let up on his torment, pulling her further and further until she was utterly spent.

Only then did Elliot cup her chin, turning her face toward his. He kissed her, deep and hard, and she rolled away from Peter and into her husband. She pushed up on her knees, digging one hand into Elliot's thick, dark hair, angling his mouth for better access as he rumbled again with pleasure. She wanted him inside of her. So desperately.

With her free hand she dragged it down his chest, finding the buttons of his fall front and loosening them. She pulled the fabric away and his big cock bounced free. She began to stroke him, over and over until he thrust up hard into her hand.

Then she looped one leg over his thigh, straddling him, bringing her wet body down over him as they groaned together in pleasure. As she began to ride him, she glanced back over her shoulder. Peter had also opened his fall front. He sat back on the bed, watching them, stroking himself with a look of pure pleasure.

Elliot lifted his head from her shoulder, and together they watched for a moment. Then he extended two fingers and beckoned Peter closer. Peter hesitated just a fraction of a moment, then came up the bed. He stood up on the mattress when he was near their heads, putting his cock where she could reach it. Merritt kissed Elliot one last time before she turned into Peter and took his cock in hand.

God, how many times had she wondered about this cock? How many times had she secretly pictured this very man over her as she stroked herself to completion? And now he was in her hand, not quite as long as her husband's cock, but thicker. She glanced at Elliot, grinding against him, building both their pleasure.

And he nodded. "Suck him," he whispered.

She didn't have to be told twice. She rode harder as she rolled her tongue over the head of Peter's cock, then took him deeper, deeper, into her throat. She swirled her tongue around him and he made a choked sound as he braced himself on the wall behind the bed.

He began to fuck her throat and she flexed harder over Elliot. Her pleasure mounted once again, this time sharper because she had already come, sharper because she knew what Elliot could do and she was ready for it.

Her husband cupped her hips, grinding her over him harder and faster as she sucked Peter into her throat. Both men were moaning now, and the sound of them in harmony was enough to push her over the edge. She bucked against Elliot's cock, her gasps and cries lost against the thickness of the cock in her mouth.

Peter dug his hand into her hair and she felt the chord of his control fray and then snap. He cried out and tried to pull away, but she gripped the base of him and let him pump into her throat as he came.

Elliot gasped at the sight. She pulled away from Peter and gazed down at her husband, his expression animal as he fucked up into her harder and faster, his hands gripping her until they would leave little bruises. When he came, he cried out her name, burying his head against her breasts as he filled her up.

She collapsed against him, his warm arms coming around her as they had a thousand times over the years. Only this time, they weren't alone. Peter sank down on the bed next to them, his weight a reminder of what they'd just done. A fantasy come true, in more ways than one.

∽

Elliot

Merritt lay in his arms, weak with pleasure. He'd seen her this way before, of course. It was one of his greatest pleasures to make her come so hard she didn't want to move but just lie with him as he stroked his fingers through her red hair.

He did so as he looked next to them. Reid lay on the bed on his side, watching the two of them. He didn't reach out, didn't touch either one of them, but Elliot felt his presence as much as if he were holding Elliot's cock.

Elliot blinked the thought away and lifted Merritt's chin to kiss her. He tasted Reid on her, salty and sweet, mixed with her own flavor and shivered. "That was remarkable."

She nodded. "Yes."

"Truly, Merry," Peter agreed, and Elliot flinched at the use of the nickname. He'd never called Merritt by the shortened version, Merry. He knew no one else who did, but that only proved the deep connection these two had once had. "Thank you both," Reid continued.

Elliot arched a brow. "Do you think we're finished?"

Merritt returned her glance to him. "I…"

"We're here a week," Elliot said. "This is for you, as long as Reid has the time. And the inclination."

Merritt sat up, her pupils dilated, but her expression uncertain. She looked at him for a long moment, then looked at Peter for even longer. Once again that potent combination of jealousy and desire put every part of Elliot on edge. He wanted Merritt to have what she wanted. He wanted to watch her come like he just had. He'd pictured that scenario many a time, but living it?

Even better.

And still, the fact that she had a connection to Reid made all this feel…dangerous. He feared it and desired it in almost equal measure.

"Elliot," she whispered.

He touched her face, tracing the line of her jaw. "Do you want this? That's the only answer that matters, Merritt."

She blinked down at him and nodded. "I…do. But it isn't the only answer that matters. Because it isn't only my decision." She looked at Reid. "Peter?"

"Merry," he whispered in return.

Elliot speared him with a sharp look. "You want her. I'm not such a fool that I can't see it written all over your face whether your tongue is buried in her while she screams or you're simply standing a room near her. So I know what you just did cannot be enough for you. You must want to feel her come around your cock. You must want to know how every inch of her skin tastes."

Reid shut his eyes and a great shudder worked through him. "Yes," he finally admitted.

Merritt's fingers dug into Elliot's shoulders at the admission and she rocked against him gently.

"And you want him to stretch you, don't you?" Elliot asked her, and reveled in how her pupils dilated with renewed desire. "To feel your legs shake around his hips like they have so many times around mine?"

She stared at him a long time, her gaze slowly narrowing as if she was trying to read some ulterior motive in him. He held there, hiding any secrets he might not wish to tell. Her lips pursed and the spark lit up in her stare.

God, how he loved seeing it there. Knowing how easily she could turn it on him and light up his entire world.

"What I want, if we're all being honest, Elliot, is to feel both of you inside of me at the same time." She arched a brow in challenge and then glanced at Peter.

Elliot did the same and found the other man staring, his cock already coming back to life at the image she created. Elliot's was doing the same. He'd never shared a woman before. Oh, how he wanted to share her.

"Very good, my lady," Elliot said softly as he smiled at her.

She shook her head slightly and then pushed from his lap and off the bed. She swept up the robe that had been left on a nearby chair by her maid and slung it over her shoulders.

"But first," she said, padding to the door without looking back at either of them, confident as a queen, "I want to eat."

CHAPTER 4

Merritt

Merritt sat at the cozy wooden table set in the corner of the cottage's kitchen, watching Elliot put together an elaborate sandwich for her across the room. Peter sat next to her, staring at the same.

"The Marquess of Egerton…makes food?" Peter finally said in an awed and confused tone.

The corner of Elliot's lips quirked briefly as he set her plate in front of her. "Only for her," he corrected, and took a long moment to look at Peter. "And only on special occasions. But for you I'll make an exception, Mr. Reid."

Elliot turned away and went back to fix his own plate and Peter's. When he returned, he sat down next to her on the other side and briefly leaned in to kiss her before they all began to eat.

She picked at her food even though her stomach rumbled, and looked back and forth at the two men who flanked her. On the surface they could not be more different: dark and light, titled and not, rich and…well, Peter couldn't exactly be called poor anymore.

He had built himself up as a sought-after playwright. Thanks to Elliot, it seemed.

Elliot arched a brow at how she wasn't eating. She playfully glared at his silent order before she took a bite of the sandwich. God, that was good. He did know what she liked. Always. And what she wanted. Which made her ponder the two of them even further.

"You know I'm still not entirely sure how we got here," she said at last. "How did you two meet and when? And how did you end up in my parlor today, Peter?"

Peter finished chewing before he spoke, a thoughtful expression on his face. "Let me see. About seven years ago I had a little play produced in a rundown theatre in one of the worst districts in London. I'd been fighting for years to have something I'd written put on and even though I knew it was a dreadful production and only a handful of people came…most of whom were drunk…I was still proud."

"As you should be," Merritt said.

"On the closing night of the production I was told, and let me quote exactly what was said…*some rich toff is here to see you.*"

Elliot smiled slightly at the description and leaned back in his chair to watch the story be told. Once again, Merritt recognized the pretended nature of his casual posture. This was Elliot on the hunt. How many times had she been the prey? But this time he was watching Peter. She shivered at the realization.

"And that rich toff was my husband?" she encouraged.

Peter nodded. "Indeed. He came to the back and told me how much he'd enjoyed the play."

"And he dared to call me a liar," Elliot interrupted. "Me."

Peter smiled this time. "Indeed, I did, I fear. Because the play was terrible, Egerton."

"The *production* was terrible," Elliot corrected softly. "The play was adequate. Though certainly not your best work."

Merritt wrinkled her brow at the easy nature of their banter. Here she'd been in the dark entirely as the two most important men in her life had apparently become...well, she wouldn't say friends. Elliot wasn't acting the way he did around those he called friend.

But something that wasn't enemies, despite the shared nature of their attraction to her.

"At any rate, he said he saw something in me," Peter said. "And he agreed to become my patron. Which changed my life."

Merritt shook her head. "But...and I am not being arrogant when I ask this."

"You?" Elliot teased gently, and she shot him a playfully dark look.

"Peter, there is no way you didn't know that Elliot was my husband. You must have known who I married."

"Of course, I did," Peter said. "Of course, I did, Merry. I was aware of every single movement you made after I was cast out of your life. I couldn't help but track them...just to...just to make certain you were well."

Merritt shifted at the idea he had been following the trajectory of her life. It was comforting somehow to realize his presence had always been there.

"I knew you'd married Egerton years before," he continued, and now his gaze moved away from hers. "I even tried to bring up the topic with your husband once after he was my patron, but was put off. So we never spoke of it."

Merritt pivoted to face Elliot straight on. "Why? Why would you approach a man I'd once cared for and then...then not discuss that shared bond?" Elliot didn't answer but shrugged lightly. She pursed her lips. "Egerton, I *know* you. You have a reason for everything you do. Why?"

For a moment she thought he might actually respond, tell the truth. It seemed to hover between the three of them, but then his expression went empty. He put up the walls he was so good at erecting to protect himself.

"Caprice," he said. Lied. She knew he lied. She just wasn't entirely certain of why.

Peter seemed just as unsatisfied by the answer, but he didn't push any more than she did. It seemed they were equally aware that Elliot could not be made to give any more than he chose to give.

"So you see, I owe your husband a great deal," Peter said softly. "And when he crooks his finger…" Now he wasn't looking at her, but at Elliot. "I come. Like I did today."

Merritt shivered at the tension that crackled between all three of them. She'd never felt anything so intense before in all her life. Even when she and Elliot went to watch at the Donville Masquerade, or slipped to one of the rooms in the back where they could be watched by strangers…she'd never felt such a powerful strain toward what they wanted.

It had the potential to be explosive, like it had been for her earlier in the evening.

"Good," she said. "I also come when he crooks his finger. Inside of me or otherwise."

Elliot shifted at her lewd description and set his napkin down on top of his half-finished plate. "Have you had your fill?" he asked her.

She held his gaze. "Of food."

"Good." He glanced toward Peter and nodded. "Then I think it's time to really begin, don't you all?"

Peter

Peter leaned against the door in the bedchamber, watching as Merritt and Elliot moved together at the foot of the bed. Their desire was so well-matched, their movements all driven to derive maximum pleasure for themselves and give the same to each other. There was a poetry to it, of an erotic kind.

Elliot untied Merry's robe as he leaned in to kiss her long, graceful neck. His fingers just glided along the edge where the fabric met skin and she hissed out a gasp of pleasure. Elliot smiled against her now naked body, like that sound was music to his ears. Peter was mesmerized by all of it.

By her, after all this time. Still and always. Only deeper now because he knew physical desire truly meant, as did she.

And by him, by Elliot. This man who moved like he always knew what he wanted. Who commanded a room with the smallest word. Only Peter knew a secret. Elliot wanted him, too. He'd always felt that coursing between them. Felt the desire that he shared. A draw toward both men and women, where pleasure was the only king.

It was certainly part of why the marquess had invited him here. Now would he do anything about it?

That was another question entirely.

Elliot was kissing Merry now, deep and probing as she sagged against him, panting in pleasure. She glanced at Peter and motioned him to her. He went, drawn like a moth to a flame. A pair of flames. Elliot didn't hesitate, but turned his wife toward Peter, even as he kept a hand possessively against her belly and stroked along her side with the other.

Peter kissed her and she whimpered against his mouth. God, but she was sweet and responsive. He wanted to touch her all over, to find all the spots that Elliot already knew so they could work them as a pair and make her come and come and come until they were all drunk on it.

He started with her breasts, cupping them as he continued to kiss her. He stroked his thumbs across her nipples and she gasped against his mouth. He lifted his gaze and found Elliot watching intently, nodding as if to encourage him to go further.

He dragged his mouth away from her lips and down her throat. As he did so, Elliot guided his own hands to her breasts. Their fingers brushed as they passed each other and Elliot's breath hitched at the grazing touch.

The marquess held her breasts up as an offering and Peter took it, licking her nipple, sucking it until she cried out and dragged her fingers into his hair to hold him steady. He teased and tormented her, loving how her hips ground against both of them in a rapidly increasing rhythm as she sought her own pleasure.

He switched to the opposite breast and repeated the torture all the more. When he pulled away, Elliot brushed his fingers against the nipple Peter had just abandoned, massaging the wetness of his tongue into her flesh as she moaned.

"Shall we have her together, as she wishes?" Elliot asked him, his voice rough and low.

Peter glanced down at her, with her eyes wide and pupils dilated. "Is she ready for that?" he asked.

"I am," she promised.

Elliot chuckled. "She likes to play," he said before he tilted Merry's face toward his and kissed her deeply again. "My sweetest, most proper marchioness loves to have her arse used. Begs for it regularly."

Peter's knees almost buckled with that revelation, but he managed to keep himself upright as Elliot pushed Merry into his arms.

"Take what you like, my lady," Elliot whispered.

Merry wrapped her arms around Peter's neck, lifting into him as she began grind against him. "You need to be naked," she growled. "It's very unfair that I'm the only naked one."

"It's very wicked," Elliot corrected as he opened a drawer beside the bed and withdrew an ornate bottle of oil. She shivered as he brought it back. "And you like being wicked. But I agree. For the next part we will all need to be naked. Who shall go first?"

She pointed at Peter. "Him. Because I've never seen him naked before."

Peter saw the marquess's cheek tighten ever so slightly. A flash of jealousy amidst the rest. It was gone as quickly as it had come. Still, Peter marked it even if he set it aside for the pleasures to come.

He returned her to Elliot's arms so he could begin undressing. He did so slowly, unfastening every button with careful determination to draw out the moment. Watching both Merry and Elliot for their reactions to the slow revelation of his body.

As he did so, Elliot poured oil onto his fingers. He moved Merry to the bed, bending her over the edge so she could keep watching Peter. His began to work his fingers against her bottom, eliciting gulping gasps from her as she continued to stare at Peter.

He had finished unwinding his cravat now and tossed it aside, then he unbuttoned his shirt. Her eyes went wide as he tugged it over his head and dropped it on the floor. But it wasn't Merry who *he* was truly watching—it was Elliot. Elliot, who was gaping at him, pupils dilated, unmoving as stared.

"Take off the rest," Merry gasped, and pushed back against Elliot at the same time, forcing his fingers into her to stretch her further.

Elliot blinked and leaned in to kiss the base of her neck, sucking gently. "Greedy, greedy."

She ground back against him and Elliot grunted low and deep from his chest. He slapped her bare arse before he reached back into the drawer where he'd found the oil and brought out a small, silky bag.

Peter moved to a chair and began to remove his boots, even as he watched what was happening between the couple with interest and desire thrumming through every nerve ending. Elliot looked at him again and slowly removed a plug from the bag. Peter knew exactly what it was and lifted his brows. It seemed the marquess had not been lying that arse play was part of their regular repertoire.

Merry moaned, lifting her backside higher in offering to her husband, her hands gripping the sheets. "Please, please."

Elliot stopped looking at Peter and put all his attention on his wife. His focused desire, pointed at Merry...it made Peter's cock twitch beneath trousers that now felt uncomfortably snug against him. He unfastened the fall front with a flick of his wrist and pushed to his feet to kick them away.

And now he was naked. Merry pushed her arms straight, lifting up to stare at him in a slow pass from head to toe. "Oh my God," she whispered.

"Indeed," Elliot murmured, his dark eyes flitting over the same path hers had. Then he went back to looking down at her offered bottom as he worked the plug inside of her slowly to stretch her, ready her, for one of their cocks.

The sound Merry made as the marquess seated the toy in her was hardly human. Her legs shook and she buckled against the bed's edge, her face disappearing into the tangled covers for a moment as she swore with the fluency a sailor would applaud.

Elliot flashed a quick, rare grin. "You see. Begs for it."

"I see," Peter whispered, and came around the bed to look at her. Elliot stepped aside, but not far, and Peter was very aware in that moment that he and Merry were entirely naked but the marquess was still entirely dressed. It felt very wicked, like they were his playthings.

And they were, he supposed. Elliot might talk about this exploration of pleasure being all for Merry, but Peter had fucked enough to know that wasn't true. The marquess had his own desires to explore.

Ones Peter was very happy to help with.

"Fuck her," Elliot murmured as he walked away, around the bed to the chair where Peter had sat to remove his boots. He slid low on the cushion and watched, hands gripping the armrests so hard that his knuckles were white.

Peter shivered. He had fantasized so often about having this woman, from the time he was old enough to know what sex was. Over the long years they were parted, he had still dreamed of burying himself in her as she wailed and twisted in pleasure beneath him, around him. And now…

Now this was fantasy about to come true.

"Merry," he began.

She glared at him over her shoulder. "You heard him. Please!"

Peter chuckled at the irritated demand, the desperate consent, and did not make her wait anymore. He wrapped an arm around her midsection, lifting her a little, positioning her so he could align his now rock-hard cock against her positively gushing entrance. She whimpered as he stroked the head of himself through the evidence of her wild desire, the evidence of Elliot coming in her earlier.

A thought that gave him a lewd thrill. He would have a little of the marquess right this moment, along with his wife. He thrust into her in one long stroke. She was so wet there was no resistance, and she cried out as he took her to the hilt.

She ground back, gripping him in a pussy so tight it felt like she'd been built to match him. She rippled, a hint of orgasm to come, and the sensation streaked up his cock. Slowly he began to grind into her, holding her hip with one hand as he glided the other to her throat.

She gripped harder when he squeezed just the slightest bit, enough to let her feel him there, not enough to hurt. Elliot made a soft sound on the chair and Peter watched as he opened his fall front and caught his cock in his hand to stroke absently as he watched them together.

And so Peter put on a show. He thrust gently, then harder, feeling the grip of her, feeling the hint of the toy in her arse with every stroke. Just like he'd feel Elliot later. God, he could come right now, just imagining that.

But he wouldn't. No, he had so much work to do before that happened. Especially when Merry shoved a hand between her thighs and began to arch against her fingers in time to his thrusts. He drew her along, edging her toward the release she clearly craved. But before he let her find it, he glanced back up at Elliot.

"Should I ready her for you?" he asked, and removed the hand from her hip to grasp the flat end of the plug. He slowly began to work it, drawing the toy nearly out of her, then easing it back in. Over and over as he thrust in time, as she humped her fingers and screamed so loud that he would wager anyone outside would hear her.

She came, gripping his cock so hard that he nearly spent. Waves of pleasure rolled through her, through him as she swore and writhed and slammed back against his cock and the toy inside of her.

He glanced up to find Elliot had removed his jacket, his waistcoat. His cravat was nearly undone as he unwrapped it at breakneck speed. Peter continued to stroke her as he watched the inevitable moment when he would see this man in all his glory.

When it finally happened, when the Marquess of Egerton stripped his shirt away and almost tore his trousers off, Peter forgot how to breathe. Elliot had always been uncommonly handsome. Peter had never been able to deny that, even from the first time he met him.

With a harsh jaw and gorgeous features, dark eyes and full lips, broad shoulders and thick thighs, no one could look at him and not think...*god*. But when he was naked?

It was all multiplied. He wasn't soft, not in any way, and when he moved across the room toward them, there was no doubt that he was in control. At least for the moment. Peter intended to test that control.

Elliot said nothing as took a place on the pillows on his back, his hard cock pointing upward, ready for her. "Take out the toy," he ordered Peter. "And Merritt? Merritt."

She lifted her head and stared at him, desire still sparking in that gorgeous blue-green sea of her gaze. "I want you in me."

"Exactly," he almost purred.

Peter did as he'd been told, gripping the toy and gently removing it. She moaned as he did so and pulled away from him. He grunted as his cock slid from her wet pussy, and took himself in hand to stroke as he watched her climb up on the bed. She cupped Elliot's face and kissed him deeply as the marquess set a possessive hand against her backside, massaging there.

At last, she parted from him with one meaningful look and then she turned her back, straddling Elliot so he could watch as she positioned herself over his cock. He helped her align her arse, and together they eased their bodies closer, moaning in unison as he took her inch by gorgeous inch.

When they were fully joined, Merry rocked against him, fucking his cock with her arse as she gripped his thighs for purchase.

Elliot let her for a moment, his eyes coming shut like he was just savoring the feel of her around him. But after a few long pumps, he opened them and speared Peter with a heated look. He reached forward and caught Merry's arms, pulling her back against his chest. She adjusted herself, lying back, lifting her legs, opening her pussy to Peter.

He didn't hesitate but moved between both their spread legs. He placed one hand on Merry's soft thigh, the other on Elliot's steely one, and felt both of them ripple with his touch. He pressed his cock back against her flexing sex and pushed. With Elliot's big cock in her it took more effort to fill her, but he did it and she twisted against them both.

"Oh my God," she wailed, grabbing for Peter's shoulders like he could give her purchase against the storm about to come.

But he wasn't here to offer salvation. Oh no. He was here to bring her to her knees, to make her beg and screech and cry out. And so he began to move, stroking his cock into her, against Elliot through her, and suddenly they weren't three people, but one desperate animal, seeking pleasure.

And finding it in a more powerful way than Peter had felt before. A way he feared he might never find again once this magical week was over.

And what a loss that would be.

CHAPTER 5

Merritt

Since marrying Elliot a decade before, Merritt had experienced pleasures beyond her wildest dreams. From the first time he touched her on their wedding night, making her come had been his pastime, his obsession, and that physical pleasure had united them. She had come so many times for him and with him, in so many ways, but this…

This moment where both Peter and Elliot filled her, where they moved in almost perfect unison so that one was always withdrawing while the other was always thrusting forward? This moment where she was only aware of the sensations tearing through her body?

She had never felt anything like it.

She gripped Peter's shoulder tighter even as she reached back to cup Elliot's cheek. He turned his mouth into her, kissing her palm as he growled. "Come for me. Come for him."

She almost laughed. There was going to be no preventing what he asked for in a moment. She felt the pleasure building in her, harder and more powerful than anything she'd ever felt before. She sank into it, not rushing it, not reaching for it, just letting it roll over her like a building storm.

When it hit, she realized she hadn't been prepared at all. Her entire body convulsed as the two men fucked harder in their own building pleasure. Wave after unstoppable wave of sensation rippled through her, offering her both unspeakable delight and unbelievable relief. Elliot's mouth met the back of her shoulder, and he kissed and lightly nipped her flesh as his moans grew louder to merge with hers.

Peter watched her, almost in wonder, like he'd never expected what was happening. Of course, neither had she, but how glad she was that they were here. That Elliot had arranged this powerful joining.

Peter's expression twisted in ecstasy and he came first, pulling from her body, letting his release splash over her hot against her stomach as he cried out her name. Elliot followed quickly behind, filling her just as he had earlier in the day, his fingers digging into her hips.

She was shaking with the power of it all, with the exhaustion of what she'd just done and who she had done it with. She hardly noticed as Peter drew her up off of Elliot, cuddling her into his side as her husband scooted away.

Fingers were stroking through her hair. Peter's or Elliot's? She wasn't entirely certain. Maybe it didn't matter. She just wanted their hands on her forever, their bodies to be hers forever.

She wanted to forget that it wasn't possible. That this was a birthday gift, a limited-time experience that had to end.

Elliot's mouth brushed along her arm gently, and she turned toward him as he wiped a tear she hadn't known she was shedding from the corner of her eye with his thumb.

"Bath?" he asked.

She blinked. Without servants he would have to fill it from the well just outside the house. In the dark of night, no less. But of course he would. Marquess or not, he was always willing to serve when it came to her.

"Yes," she whispered. "As long as you'll be part of it."

He smiled, though there was a little distance to his stare as he pushed from the bed.

"Do you want my help?" Peter asked.

Elliot looked at him briefly as he grabbed his trousers, then turned away to tug them on. "No. You take care of her."

Peter hesitated, then nodded. She cuddled closer to him, even as she watched Elliot go to the bedchamber door. There he paused, looked at them for a long moment.

And then he was gone. And she was alone with Peter for the first time since she'd found him in her parlor earlier in the day. Only they hadn't truly been alone then, of course. That was all Elliot's machinations to begin this game. Now they were truly alone, and probably would be for a while.

She glanced up at Peter, drinking in the sight of his blond locks, tangled from her fingers. She stroked his chest and the little curls there.

"Are we going to talk about…about us?" she asked.

He tensed a little, as if he recognized the danger in that subject as much as she did. "Eventually we'll have to, I think."

Quiet hung between them, both a comfort and not. Eventually, she cleared her throat. "I-I never stopped thinking of you."

"Nor I you," he said, his hands smoothing against her back. "In the beginning, I used to drive my phaeton past your estate near St. James Park and just…hope to catch a glimpse of you."

She wrinkled her brow as she continued to stare up at him. "And did you?"

"Sometimes," he said. "But it always made it hurt more. So I stopped after a while."

"Well, you had much to keep you busy," she said, pushing aside the sad emotions this conversation stirred in her. The ones that felt like a betrayal of her husband. "After all, you have become very successful."

"Thanks in part to the marquess, of course," Peter said.

"Yes, I suppose so. We three have been inextricably bound for longer than I ever knew. And now Elliot has brought you to me." She shivered. "I hardly know what to feel."

"It seems you have had a happy life with him, though," Peter said. "Your physical compatibility is evident even when you touch each other in a glancing way."

She nodded. Under any other circumstances, it would feel...*wrong* to talk about her private, physical relationship with her husband. Especially to another man. But since they were all sharing in such sinful activities together, she didn't hold back.

"You and I had only ever kissed, so I was such an innocent when we married," she said with a faint smile. She would hardly recognize that nervous girl now. "And Elliot was patient but determined to learn every facet of my pleasure. And help me learn them too. Passion has never been our problem. In fact, it has often solved a great many others."

"Such as?"

She worried her lip as she thought of those early days after the marriage when she'd felt so lost. "When I realized I could so entirely trust that man with my body, that he would never do anything to hurt me, that he would always seek my enthusiastic consent and shattering pleasure...I was able to trust him in other ways. In every way."

Peter nodded slowly. "Good. I admit that when I found out your father was marrying you off to a title, I feared that your happiness would be threatened. So the fact that you have been happy with the marquess is a relief."

"And what about you? What about your *happiness*?" She gave him a teasing wink. "I've heard that you find a great deal of it all over London and as your success grows are a sought-after companion in the receiving room *and* the bedroom."

"Ah, so you are researching my romantic life, are you?" he asked with a laugh. "Were you scandalized?"

"First off, you are not particularly discreet, so there is little research involved," Merritt said, and felt no jealousy now. Had there been before she'd been allowed to experience the pleasures of his flesh? Perhaps. But now? No. "And I was…*titillated*. You seem to have a vast appetite for sin."

He shrugged. "I think I always did, though I did my best to wedge that desire into what I was told was a palatable direction. Eventually, though, my mindset changed. After all, I had done everything I was supposed to do and yet was denied. Once your father pushed me out into the world, I stopped giving a damn so much what others thought of me. And yes, I experimented over the years, followed my desire to whatever woman…or man…it took me to. Is that what you mean by a vast appetite?"

She sat up and looked at him. "Yes, I suppose it is."

"And that shocked you?" he asked softly.

She shook her head. "No. Elliot and I have a lifetime membership to the Donville Masquerade and we explore erotic texts together. We've seen what a wide variety of pleasures there can be, even if we haven't involved ourselves in all of them. I know that men can desire men. They can desire men and women individually and together, and express those desires in a variety of ways. As can women. I've only ever found such expressions to be arousing, not shocking."

There was relief that flooded Peter's face and she realized he'd believed she might judge him for his desires. But she didn't. She only felt curiosity about them…probably because they made her take a fuller accounting of her husband.

Elliot had watched Peter with as much interest as she had during this powerful day together. When Peter had touched him as they all came together just moments before, she'd felt the marquess react with pleasure. She'd wondered before if Elliot shared the same proclivities that Peter had just admitted to.

Now she questioned that fact even more. Found herself titillated by the potential answer. What would it be like to watch her husband, the man of great control, the man who never fully gave over…be taken by Peter? Be pleasured by Peter. And offer his wealth of talents at giving pleasure in return.

Her body twitched with renewed desire.

Peter tugged her back into his arms and sighed. "Rest now, Merry. We'll have plenty of time to discuss our pasts, but I think your husband has a great deal in store for us in the next few days. You'll need all your strength for that."

She nodded and closed her eyes. Exhaustion washed over her with the same overpowering wave as pleasure had shortly before. And she gave in to it, fading into sleep and dreams that were now just an echo of how erotic her reality had become.

CHAPTER 6

Peter

Peter stepped outside into the cooler night air and caught his breath. Elliot was coming toward the house, a bucket of water in each hand. He had not put on a shirt, so the flexing muscles of his arms were clearly outlined in the moonlight that fell over him and made him look like a dark fallen angel.

"I thought I told you to take care of her," Elliot snapped as he reached Peter, forced to raise his voice over the sound of the roaring sea just below them.

Peter didn't ask for permission, but simply took one of the buckets from the marquess's hand. "She is asleep," he explained.

Elliot's cheek twitched and he entered the house. Peter shook his head as he followed. Apparently the marquess was back to being the distant patron rather than the passionate lover who couldn't take his eyes off Peter's body.

He followed Elliot into the kitchen where a large pot of water was boiling. Elliot removed it from the fire, filled a second pot with water from his bucket and then placed it over the flames.

He arched a brow at Peter. "Bring that bucket of cold and follow me."

Peter inclined his head. "Yes, *my lord.*"

Elliot's eyes narrowed, but he didn't respond, simply took the back stair out of the kitchen and up to the hallway. They entered the dressing chamber that was attached to the bedchamber where Merry slept. A huge tub was set in the middle. Huge, certainly big enough for two, and it was already more than half-full from the marquess's efforts. He poured the boiling water in and the tub steamed.

"Pour yours in," Elliot directed.

Peter did as he'd been told, pouring slowly as Elliot tested the water so it wouldn't become too cold. When he'd poured about two-thirds of the bucket in, Elliot nodded.

"That will be enough," he said. "And the water boiling downstairs can reheat it if she needs it. Or to wash ourselves after she's finished."

"You think of everything," Peter said softly.

Elliot lifted his gaze. "When it comes to her, I try." He shook his head.

"Which is why you brought me here."

Elliot didn't answer for a moment, just grabbed one of the towels stacked in a huge pile in the corner of the room and wiped the sweat from his chest after the exertion of filling the tub. Peter stared at him as he did it. He would love to follow the path of that towel with his tongue. What would the very proper Marquess of Egerton do then?

Peter had some idea. And it was explosive.

"I read about your parting from the letters between our fathers, as I said earlier in the day," Elliot said. "But I never heard her side of the story, as I never brought it up. I've never heard the truth at all, I would wager, since her father was a terrible piece of shit who only cared for himself."

Peter pursed his lips. He supposed if anyone had the right to know their story, it was Egerton. Not that he relished the retelling and all the pain it brought back up.

He ran a hand through his hair and began, "My father worked for hers. We grew up together. And grew to..." He hesitated. He would say love, but maybe not to this man. "We grew to care for each other."

Elliot's nostrils flared, as if he already knew the part Peter had withheld, but he made no corrections.

"I would have married her. I *wanted* to marry her." Peter caught his breath at the truth of that statement. "But her father caught wind of our feelings. He was enraged. To him, Merry was a tool, something to be bargained with and I, the son of a servant, could offer him no benefit. Though I suppose that isn't uncommon in men of your rank."

Elliot tilted his head. "I suppose not."

"When he confronted me, he brought my father into the room. And it became clear that they were on the same side. I was pushed out. Expelled from the house with the threat that my father could be destroyed and Merry could be sold off to the worst of her potential suitors if I didn't fall in line."

"And yet you didn't pursue her?" Elliot asked, and he sounded incredulous. "Had someone threatened to take her from me, I would have moved the moon and stars to have her."

"And you have the resources to do both," Peter said. "I had not a farthing to my name. I would have starved had I not had a few friends willing to take me in, and eventually a patron to support me until I began to make my own way."

Elliot drew a long breath. "I suppose I can't say I understand because I have never been in that position. And I cannot say I'm sorry, either, because your loss, painful as it must have been, was my gain."

"And hers," Peter admitted. "You have given her a life I never could have. She is obviously happy, Egerton." He moved closer. "Elliot."

Elliot swallowed hard at this first use of his given name. Peter could taste it on his tongue, the same flavor he'd tasted on Merry earlier. How he wanted to kiss this man. To feel him buckle beneath the desires he was so clearly suppressing.

But Elliot stepped away, looked away. "And do you still love her?"

Peter froze at the question. The one he tried not to ask himself over the years. The one he refused to face when he touched her.

"How could one not?" he finally said.

Elliot nodded and turned his head, like the admission was a physical assault. "I should get her before the bath gets cold," he said, his tone choked.

Peter waved him toward the door that separated the chambers. "You do that. I'll go take the water off the fire downstairs and join you shortly."

Elliot stared at him, their gazes holding, a thousand jealousies and desires pulsing between them just like Merry's body had so recently. Finally, Elliot moved toward him and lifted a hand to press against his chest. Peter felt the weight of every finger through the linen shirt he'd slung back on when he left the bed.

"Do," was all he said as he moved his gaze from Peter's face down to where his hand touched him. Then he pulled away and opened the door to fetch Merry.

Leaving Peter's mind spinning and a thousand plans for what to do next swirling in his mind.

Elliot

Merritt was asleep, just as Peter had claimed she would be as Elliot walked into the room. Just as well. He needed a moment to make his hands stop shaking before he went to her.

His body burned with jealousy after Peter's simply recounting of a past that had colored Elliot's entire existence with Merry. That would color his future with her forever. Jealousy that Peter could so easily say that he loved her. And jealousy because he feared Merritt still felt the same.

But mixed with that jealousy, that resentment, that fear was something else. Something that froze him as much as the first emotion.

Desire.

Oh yes, there was desire for Peter Reid. He could admit that to himself, even if he never dared to do so to anyone else. Even if he'd been denying this part of himself all his life, because of the late marquess's thoughts on what Elliot should be.

"Except that he is long dead now," Elliot murmured to himself as his gaze moved to Merritt. She was tangled in the covers, one long leg draped sensually over them. He'd told her over and over today that he'd brought Peter here to give her a chance to experience what she desired. What she'd lost.

But that wasn't entirely the reason, was it? Elliot knew, deep down in his soul, that he'd picked Peter because *he* wanted the play-wright. Because there was a spark that flashed between them any time they were in a room together. Because when Peter looked at him, all he could picture was the other man's mouth closing around his length while he shook with pleasure.

Was this his chance too?

"Peter?" Merritt murmured, lifting her head.

The desire extinguished at that name. She was looking for her first love, not the man she had married. Because Elliot had opened a Pandora's Box that he likely couldn't close.

He moved to her. "No, my lady. It's me."

She smiled up at him, lifting her arms to wrap them around his neck and draw her to him. His mouth found hers and they kissed, she with lazy, sleepy desire, he with a more driven hunger. He was half-hard again by the time he parted from her, staring into her lovely face and trying to memorize every line of it.

"Ready for your bath?" he asked as he tucked his arms beneath her legs and lifted her. She rested her head against his shoulder, her hand sliding up his bare chest as her naked curves molded to him.

"Mmmm-hmmmm," she sighed.

They entered the dressing room and he set her on her feet. He stole one last kiss, letting his hands trace the length of her sides as she shivered and whispered his name against his lips. Then he extended a hand and helped her balance as she stepped into the luxurious tub that was obviously made for two.

"Going to join me?" she asked, more awake now as she scooted to the back of the big tub and opened her legs to create space. And seduction. There was no denying the glint of seduction in her blue-green stare.

"Maybe in a moment," he said, handing over soap and a cloth. He sat down in a chair next to the tub and leaned forward, resting his arms on the edge and his head on his arms so he could just...watch her.

He'd always loved watching her in the water, whether it was a tub or a lake or the sea. Her naked curves gliding through the waves put him to mind of some glorious water nymph. Or a mermaid from seafaring tales. She would sing him to his death, perhaps.

But what a way to go.

She washed herself slowly, making an obvious show for him as she soaped her breasts, her arms, down below the body to her stomach and between her legs as the water became foggy and he could no longer spy on her. She lifted a wet hand to his cheek, letting droplets follow the line of it as she smiled up at him.

"Please join me, Egerton," she murmured.

He arched a brow. "You don't want Peter to join you? He'll be up in a moment."

A little shadow crossed her expression at the question. Her gaze darted to the door, then back to him. He felt the answer in her actions even if she denied it in her words.

"I want *you* to join me, Elliot," she whispered, and caught his hand to tug him toward her.

He sighed before he kicked out of his trousers and stepped into the warm water. He let out a groan of pleasure as he sank beneath the waves. They shifted around so she was behind him and his back pressed to her front. Her arms came around him and she slowly began to rub the washcloth over his chest. Down his stomach. Around his cock, washing away the earlier activities and the sweat from filling the tub.

"Elliot," she whispered.

He turned his face toward hers slightly and their eyes met. But before she could say anything further, Peter reentered the room. There was an electricity that sparked in her when the other man moved toward them. Elliot supposed it sparked in him, as well. Peter took the chair he had abandoned and leaned back in it, watching them for a moment.

Watched Merritt, holding her gaze evenly until she flexed ever so slightly against Elliot, like Peter had called to her pleasure. He sighed as he rubbed a hand against her leg.

"As much as I would like to continue what just started again when Mr. Reid came into the room, it's been a very long day, Merritt. When we finish here, it might be best to sleep. Start again tomorrow after you've rested."

She sucked in a breath. "Elliot!"

He sat up and turned more fully toward her. "I've seen you push yourself too far with pleasure and suffer for it later. We still have six days after this to explore every single thing you wish to explore."

"Elliot is right," Peter said softly. "I'm not going anywhere."

Merritt stuck out her bottom lip in the prettiest pout that Elliot wanted to nip with his teeth. That he wanted to slap her gorgeous backside for exposing. Instead he arched a brow at her.

She sighed. "Very well, I suppose you are right. I never sleep well the night before a road trip and we were up so very early. Rest will be for the best after we finish cleaning up. But I will expect to be rewarded for my good behavior tomorrow."

Elliot cupped her cheeks and leaned in, tracing her lips with his tongue before he delved into a deep kiss. When they parted, her expression was slightly dazed with renewed passion.

"I promise you, Merritt, it will be something you never forget."

She seemed satisfied by that answer. Or as satisfied as she could be considering she was being denied. And she sank back in the tub and finished washing herself, as did Elliot.

But he recognized that her gaze kept returning to Peter. That Peter's eyes couldn't seem to leave her. That he was, in these charged moments, the odd man out of their connection. He'd known that might happen when he'd brought Peter here. He just couldn't resist giving her what she wanted.

He wouldn't stop now, even if it meant he might lose some part of her...or even all of her...in the end.

CHAPTER 7

Merritt

Merritt could feel the rays of sunshine against her eyelids even before she opened them, and she sighed as she slowly woke up from the most delicious dreams. Her body ached after all the exertion yesterday, but it was a wonderful ache. One that reminded her she had been well-loved by the two men in her bed.

That she would be well-loved all over again today.

As if to accentuate that fact, Elliot slung his arm around her from behind, tucking her back against his hard body with a drowsy sigh. She cuddled against him, enjoying the feel of him for a moment. She loved these sleepy mornings they shared together, when his hands would rove over her, his lips and eventually he'd fill her and make her come.

And sometimes he wouldn't do any of those things, but just hold her close, like she was his most valued treasure. Murmur in her ear about their life together, about his interests or whatever he had done the previous day.

The mornings were when she usually found him most open,

closest to her. Like the controlled marquess took longer to wake than the warm and caring man who was only called Elliot.

She sighed and rocked against him a little more, rubbing her backside against his naked cock. He was awake now. She felt it in the tension that entered his body, felt it when his hand tightened against one breast and he began to flick her nipple with his thumb. His cock grew hard against her.

She reached around to place a hand on his naked hip, gliding her thumb along the ridge of bone there, tracing the muscle. He made a soft sound before he pushed her hair aside and buried his mouth against the back of her neck.

He took his time with her, as if they had all day. As if Peter wasn't in the bed with them. She opened her eyes to look at the other man, and smiled to find him sprawled out on his stomach, still sleeping.

Elliot's hand stole between her legs now and she whimpered softly as he spread her folds and stroked her clitoris gently. She rested her head back, turning her face so he could kiss her. He did so, circling her endlessly as she shivered with pleasure.

He pulled away from her mouth and looked down at her. She nodded, lifting her backside a little, spreading herself open for him. He aligned his cock to her entrance and pulsed forward, filling her slowly so she could truly feel the stretch of him in her aching body. She flexed around him with a soft sigh and shut her eyes as he began to thrust, gently and with no sense of urgency. His fingers continued to circle her, creating pleasure that made her feel heavy and almost drunk on it and him.

It went on like that for a little while, them moving together like a soft wave on the ocean, not reaching for pleasure, but well-versed enough in each other's bodies to know they would find it. When she opened her eyes again she found that Peter had moved.

He now lay on his side facing them and he was watching, pupils dilated with desire. He had pushed the covers away and was stroking himself. She looked back and found Elliot watching him, too, just as he had been every time they were together.

Peter smiled and tugged the covers away from them, too, so he could truly watch. She caught his hand before he could move it away and set it on her hip, next to where Elliot gripped her. She felt her husband increase his strokes at the action, then ease back into the previous lazy rhythm.

"Fuck," Peter said softly, the only sound in the room except for the wet slapping sound of their joined bodies. "May I?"

She nodded and she felt Elliot doing the same behind her. She held her breath as Peter scooted closer and dragged his tongue over her breast. Elliot pressed his mouth to the side of her neck, watching as Peter licked and sucked her. The lazy pleasure became sharp between her legs and she bucked back against Elliot with a little moan.

"More?" Elliot whispered against her ear, his breath warm and sparking tingles in her body.

She nodded as she rocked against him and placed her hand on the back of Peter's head. He glanced up at her and gave her the most wicked grin before he started to trail lower, his tongue tracing her ribcage, her stomach, her hip.

Elliot slowed his thrusts as Peter pushed her legs open wider. She crooked one over Elliot's hip and they were fully exposed now. Peter smiled.

"What a pretty sight this is for the morning," he said softly, nodding toward where their bodies were joined and Elliot's fingers were pressed against her clitoris.

Peter reached out and touched her there too. Touched Elliot's wet fingers. Elliot moved them, but slowly and once again he thrust harder for a fraction of a moment, as if Peter's involvement made him lose that famous control he gripped so tightly.

Peter leaned in, brushing his rough cheek against Merritt's thigh, licking there as he watched her husband fuck her up close. Then he lifted into her and licked her clitoris.

Both she and Elliot froze at the action. She whimpered ever so slightly as she looked down at him, head burrowed between her thighs, tongue working slowly and methodically against her, just fractions of an inch from her husband's hard cock.

"Don't stop," she murmured, reaching up to touch Elliot's face. She was talking to him, she was talking to Peter, she was talking to herself. They were entering new territory now. She knew it, she believed both the men knew it. And she definitely didn't want to stop.

Elliot stroked again, thrusting with more purpose than before. And she felt Peter smile against her pussy as he licked and sucked harder and faster. They were working in earnest now, tandem seekers of her ultimate pleasure, and she saw it coming, felt it in the rising sensations between her legs that spread out through her entire trembling body.

She gripped the back of Peter's head harder, pushing back against Elliot's grinding cock with further abandon. They held her, sandwiched between them, working her body for the same purpose. When she came, it was sharp and sudden, like a cup that had suddenly overflowed.

She shook, trembling out of control, and in the process Elliot's cock slipped from her. She whimpered at the loss of him filling her, but before he could readjust and push back inside, Peter caught him in hand.

She stared down at him as he stroked Elliot once before he aligned him and fed him back inside her body. Elliot cried out and his hand dug into her skin. To her surprise, that thin wire of control in him snapped and he began to fuck her hard. She was still convulsing from her orgasm and his hard and heavy thrusts served to drag that pleasure out.

Peter chased their ever-moving bodies, continuing to tongue her, moaning like he was deriving as much pleasure as they were. At last Elliot groaned once more and he poured into her, overflowing her with his pleasure. It didn't stop Peter, he kept licking, cleaning away the evidence of her pleasure and her husband's until her twitching body finally collapsed in pure satisfied exhaustion.

For a brief moment they all lay there, staring at each other, taking in what had just happened. Then Elliot pulled out of her and got up, snatching up his dressing gown from the bottom of the bed.

"I'll find food," he muttered before he turned on his heel and left the room. Left them. Left what had just happened and all that would change because of it.

~

Elliot

Elliot entered the parlor downstairs without even fully realizing how he'd gotten there. His mind was racing, his body shaking as what had just happened sank in.

Peter had touched him. Grabbed his cock with certainty and beautiful, perfect pressure, stroked him. Licked him. He'd definitely felt the other man's tongue against the base of his cock while Elliot fucked Merritt. And he had *reveled* in it.

The itch he'd felt, always felt, in the back of his mind when it came to men…Peter had dragged it forward, out into the light. Made it a full-born ache.

And he wanted more. Even though he didn't know exactly what that meant. Oh, he knew what it meant physically, of course. He could easily picture a hundred scenarios with Peter without even trying hard. But what did it mean for his life? For how he saw himself? For his future with Merritt?

"Fuck, what does *any* of this mean for my future with her?" he muttered as he walked to the sideboard and poured himself a tall glass of Scottish whisky. He took a swig of it and let it burn down his throat.

"Isn't it a little early for that?"

He hesitated at the sound of Merritt's voice behind him. Slowly he turned and found her, wrapped in her dressing gown, hair mussed from being well-fucked not five minutes before. She wasn't alone, either. Peter stood behind her, dressed only in trousers that hung dangerously low on his hips. No shirt, of course; no boots, of course. His cheeks slashed by stubble that Elliot knew would feel so fucking good against his thighs. Hair sticking up from where Merritt had clung to him while he made her come with his tongue.

Exactly what Elliot would do if Peter had been between *his* legs.

"My head is already spinning," Elliot said. "Why not help it along? Besides, it's hardly early. We've slept half the morning away and fucked the rest."

Merritt met his gaze. She didn't turn away, and in that moment Elliot felt…exposed. He'd always been so good at putting up walls to his emotions, even with her. He'd been trained to do so his entire life.

But in that moment he felt stripped as naked as he was under his dressing gown.

"Elliot," she said softly, crossing the room to him. She took the drink from his hand. She set it on the sideboard with a clink and then cupped his cheeks. "I have known for a very long time that you are…interested in men."

He tensed and tried to keep his tone neutral. "Have you?"

She nodded. "You said to me at the very beginning of this that you knew me. That you could feel what I desired because we have always been so open about pleasure and need. So please don't underestimate me and think I can't do the very same thing when it comes to you."

He stared at her a moment, her fiery red hair around her shoulders, her blue-green eyes never hesitating as they held his. She was nothing but acceptance and grace in that moment. And he had never loved her more. It had never frightened him more to feel that feeling that he always tried to push aside and write off as folly. Something that a man in his position didn't pursue.

He swallowed. "I would never be so foolish as to underestimate you, my lady," he said. "But what I want or don't want…it isn't even something I understand."

She opened her mouth as if to say something more, but Peter stepped forward. "Merry, give us a moment."

She blinked up at Elliot for a beat before she turned toward him. "But I—"

Peter shook his head and came to her, taking her hands and lifting them to kiss each one in turn. "Just a moment. Please."

Elliot recognized her expression of annoyance. Like the true lady of the manor that she was, Merritt had never liked being left out of important life decisions. Yet she didn't argue with Peter, as she might have done with Elliot. She simply inclined her head and said, "Then *I* will find food."

She pivoted back to Elliot and smiled at him gently before she lifted up and kissed him. Then she stepped from the room and shut the door behind herself.

Leaving Elliot alone with the subject of his vexation, of his jealousy…of his desire. All were troubling emotions to have boiling in his chest all at once.

"When I first accepted what I am," Peter said gently, "it was odd. After all, we are raised that there is only one path upon which desire must flow." He motioned his head toward the door where Merritt had just left. "Toward her. Toward others like *her.*"

"And it does," Elliot said, and meant it with all his heart and soul. "Always. Forever."

"Of course it does," Peter said. "No one could watch you together and not know that your attraction to her is powerful and real and complete. But desire isn't a river—there isn't only one inlet and outlet, one direction to move." He moved to the window and pulled back the curtain. In the distance, the bright blue ocean sparkled in the sunshine. "It is more like the sea. It comes and goes, it rises and falls. It swirls and draws us to wherever it pleases. There is *nothing* wrong with a river. There is nothing wrong with the sea."

Elliot choked on a humorless laugh. "And when did you know that you were a…a seafaring man?"

Peter smiled. "Shall we drop the metaphor?"

"Perhaps it would be easier."

"When I was tossed out of Merry's house, I was devastated." Peter's gaze grew troubled. "To lose her, to lose the future I'd begun to hope for, to lose the life I'd always known…"

Elliot felt this Peter's pain. And beneath it, this man's love for Merritt. One that hadn't died, no matter how many years stretched between them.

Peter continued, "But in the end, the world opened up for me. I found freedom, including in the desires I'd tried to repress my entire life. I began to work in a theatre and one night, in the wings, while a soprano was singing an aria for the ages…one of the actors came to stand beside me. I'd told myself for weeks that I only admired him. That I was interested in his talents and nothing else. That was why I couldn't stop thinking about him, dreaming about him. But when he reached out to take my hand, when he pressed me against the curtains and kissed me…I knew. I knew the truth that had always been there."

Elliot shivered at the image. At the memories it sparked. "When I was younger, my fantasies when I pulled myself off were always of both men and women. But everything around me, every message I received made it very clear to me that it would be unacceptable for the first son of a marquess to enter such dangerous areas. I pushed that desire away. And then there was Merritt. And I knew she would be enough for me. She *is* enough."

"It's not about enough," Peter whispered. "It's about being who you truly are. For some that only means accepting that attraction isn't limited. They never do a thing about it, just as a man only attracted to women may be entirely faithful to one, but notice others in a fleeting way."

Elliot nodded. That made sense. Passing attraction was very different than acting on it.

Peter stepped toward him, closing some of the distance that separated them. Elliot's heart seemed to leap into his throat and he recognized with a powerful certainty that this was *not* a passing attraction.

"For others, they must act. They need to act." Peter reached out and slid his fingers along the edge of Elliot's dressing gown. His short cut and perfectly manicured nails lightly abraded the skin beneath. "I need to act, Elliot. And judging from the way you surged into my hand today when I touched you, you want to act, too. You *need* to act."

Elliot could hear the breath gasping in and out of his lungs. Peter was so close he could smell the clean scent of his skin, mixed with the earthiness of Merritt that still clung to his lips. He wanted to taste that on Peter. He wanted to taste himself and her and Peter all at once.

Peter seemed to understand that unspoken truth. Seemed to understand that Elliot couldn't yet be the one who moved, despite a lifetime of taking control when it came to desire.

Peter gripped the edge of the dressing gown and tugged Elliot against him. His mouth grazed Elliot's chin, his jaw, his cheek, and finally Peter took his lips.

CHAPTER 8

Peter

Peter had kissed a great many people in his life, both men and women. But as he took Elliot's lips, he recognized that this was more than a kiss. It felt like coming home. And that had only ever happened with one other person: Merry.

Elliot moaned against his mouth and Peter drove forward, pushing away the emotions that took him off guard even as he pushed his tongue into Elliot's mouth. The marquess sucked it greedily, his arms coming around Peter, his hands gripping against the bare skin of his back.

It was a crushing meeting now, a war for passion. Elliot pushed him back until they hit the wall and held him there, driving into him like he could lose himself forever. Like he wanted to.

After a few minutes, the kiss slowed, Elliot's fingers loosened a little against his skin. Peter moved him, switching their positions. He leaned into the marquess, feeling the pulse of Elliot's cock beneath his dressing gown. Peter so wanted to slide his hand beneath and stroke him, drop to his knees and suck him, turn him around and fill his arse until they both spent.

But he could be patient. Wait until Elliot was so needy that he would cross the barriers of his hesitations easily. So Peter kissed him once more, gently and then stepped back.

"Come now, my lord. I believe your wife is waiting for us in the kitchen. Let's eat."

Elliot blinked at him, like he was trying to understand what was happening. Then he nodded. "Very well."

Peter turned and padded from the room, feeling Elliot behind him with every step. They made their way silently to the kitchen. When they entered, Merry, who had been preparing their plates, jolted and came toward them.

"Elliot," she said.

Peter stifled a smile. Her concern was so clear. That drive to protect Elliot. Not Peter. But then again, he didn't really need protection anymore.

"I'm fine," Elliot said, but his voice trembled as he sat down at the kitchen table and stared at the plate she had prepared.

"So what did you…decide?" she asked softly.

Peter leaned in and kissed her, feeling Elliot watch them. "That we have all the time in the world," he said as he parted from her and sat down across from Elliot. She sat at the head of the table and they ate together.

Peter steered the conversation, drawing them all away from the questions and desires that had flowed between them since his arrival here. Instead they spoke of theatre and music, books and art. He felt both his lovers relax as they did so. Elliot even cracked the hint of a smile here and there, mostly when Merry became animated about a subject, which was often.

It was comfortable. Not that Peter wasn't fully aware of both of them, not that he didn't crave the little glimpses of bare skin through each of their dressing gowns.

But waiting, though difficult, sometimes made the ultimate surrender all the better. And he was certain that would soon enough be proven true once again.

~

Merritt

The sea was gentle as Merritt walked along the sandy shores in her bare feet, her gown bound up around her knees so that the water didn't weigh her down when it lapped around her toes. The afternoon had been…comfortable. Casual even, at least on the surface. After they ate, they'd all gotten dressed with only a little bit of touching and teasing and come down to the water's edge.

They'd walked together a while, a chatty threesome that would have seemed very innocent if caught this way. Only Merritt could still feel the tingle of the morning between her legs. And when she glanced back over her shoulder, she still saw the tension between Peter and Elliot.

They stood together at the edge of the bluff, watching her. And yet they were clearly very aware of each other. Elliot was turned into Peter, and Peter occasionally let his fingers play along Elliot's. A tease. A temptation.

And a fire was building with every single little grazing touch.

Merritt still had no idea what they had discussed when she was out of the room. What they had done. But she shivered every time she imagined it and what would happen next.

Peter raised a hand, motioning her back, and she moved their way. As she did so, Peter pressed a hand against Elliot's chest and leaned in, his mouth close to her husband's ear. He said something and Elliot shuddered from head to toe, his expression one she recognized very well: pure desire.

She reached them and let one hand settle on Peter's chest as she edged her way up to Elliot. She kissed her husband and he murmured her name against his lips. When they parted, he looked troubled, glancing back and forth between her and Peter.

"Will it change us?" he asked, speaking to her rather than Peter.

She knew what he meant. She knew what he feared on some

level. She'd felt the same when he offered Peter up to her, and yet…
it had only brought good things. Powerful things.

She took his hand and lifted it to her chest, holding it so he
could feel the skip of her heart beneath his fingers. "Yes," she said.
"Of course it will. But change isn't always bad, is it? We will grow
from it." She leaned even closer, her lips a whisper from his. "And
when I imagine what you two will do to each other, I can hardly
keep from touching myself. Touching you."

Elliot held her stare for a moment and then nodded toward
Peter. "Then I want this. I want to go back inside and have you both.
Truly have you."

Peter caught each of their hands in his and tugged them toward
the cottage. "Then let's go."

Elliot

T he Marquess of Egerton was not accustomed to being rushed
and pushed, and yet that was exactly what was happening as
the three of them all but tumbled up the stairs toward the bedroom.

Elliot had maintained a tight grip on control his entire life. And
he kept that grip even with Merritt, used it as a guiding principle in
seduction. But right now he didn't feel like the one in charge.

Because he had no idea what to do next or how to feel about
what was about to happen. Thrilled, excited…afraid. All those
emotions swirled in him, along with the recognition that what was
about to happen would be a point of no return. There would be a
before…and an after, this afternoon in their bed.

"Stop thinking, my lord," Peter said, his tone suddenly sharp as
he shut the door and turned to Elliot and Merritt.

Elliot narrowed his gaze. "Am I so obvious?"

"So obvious. But the time for thinking is over. Now it is time to
feel. To let me help you feel."

"I know how to feel," Elliot snapped.

Peter arched a brow. It was an accusation without words and Elliot folded his arms in response. Peter huffed out a breath and rushed across the room, cupping Elliot's cheeks and kissing him. The kiss was forceful, driven, and all the thoughts Peter had been trying to erase fell away from Elliot's mind. Desire coursed through him instead, hard and harsh and sharp as a blade through every vein.

Peter pulled back. "*Stop thinking,*" he whispered. "And sit down on the settee."

Another order and this time Elliot didn't fight it. He did as he was told, sitting in the middle of the settee before the fire, widening his legs to sprawl.

Merritt had been staring at the two of them, and now Peter turned his attention to her. He stepped up to her and without a word stripped open the buttons along the front of her gown in one easy flick of his wrist. She gasped as he yanked the fabric open and down, baring her from the waist up. He bent his head, watching Elliot from the corner of his eye as he sucked one nipple and she all but collapsed into his mouth.

Elliot shifted, his cock hardening at the rough display of passion. At the way Merritt ground up, already excited, already finding pleasure before anyone even touched her. God, how he loved watching her come. Making her come. Tasting her come.

There was nothing better.

It seemed Peter agreed. He shoved her gown the rest of the way down and there she was: naked. Peter reached between her legs as he kept kissing her and gave a low chuckle. "Wet," he said to Elliot as he withdrew dewy fingers. "Want to taste?"

Elliot nodded, and Peter set her aside to return to him on the settee. He traced his fingers along Elliot's lips and then let him lick them clean. He was in control now, and yet Elliot recognized the ripple when he sucked the other man's fingers. Control could be broken by pleasure.

"Now then," Peter said, and crooked a finger at Merritt. "Here is what you will do. You're going to fuck your husband."

Her brow wrinkled. "Er…"

"Oh yes, we'll get to my fun. In time. But first you need to get him ready for me. I want you to pull his cock free, make him beg for you and fuck him while I watch you."

Elliot flexed his hips, almost against his will, as if he could reach Merritt across the room. She looked up at Peter, but then her gaze shifted to Elliot. There was a light in her eyes, a wicked glimmer he didn't think he'd ever seen, and he had made a study of Merritt in all manner of debauchery.

This was Merritt on a mission. And the way she sauntered across the room toward him, her gaze fixed firmly on his, could have unmanned him all on its own.

She leaned over him, bracing her hands on the back of the settee and brushing her breasts against his lips. He darted out his tongue, tasting her in the same place Peter had, loving how she hissed out pleasure at just that little touch.

She tugged at his shirt and he unbuttoned just enough to pull it over his head. Then she unfastened his trousers. He was hard already, of course he was after the last few hours of teasing stimulation. Of fantasy about to come to life.

Merritt was certainly part of that fantasy as she took him firmly in hand and stroked him. Over and over. Harder and then softer, faster then slower. Teasing him.

"Take them off," she ordered.

He nodded and lifted his hips against her as he shed his trousers.

"Show me how he likes to be sucked," Peter said.

Elliot jolted as he looked across the room. Peter had taken up a position on one of the chairs just out of reach. He leaned forward, watching them through a glittering gaze.

Merritt looked toward him and nodded. She smiled at Elliot before she dropped to her knees and took him into her mouth. He groaned at the lightning pleasure she instantaneously created. No one was better than her at sucking him off. She knew every way to lick and fuck and swirl and suck that made his vision blur and his balls empty. She played all her tricks, watching him as he grunted and lifted into her throat until she gasped for air.

He could have spent a lifetime in her mouth, only that wasn't enough for Peter. He snapped his fingers, his breath short as he growled, "Now ride him for me."

She didn't hesitate, but lifted from her knees in one smooth motion. She lowered her body over Elliot, heat and wetness encasing him as she crashed down over him in one heavy thrust. She moaned as she began to grind, riding him for her pleasure, using him like he was nothing more than one of her toys stuffed into her bedside drawer back in London.

He cupped her hips, helping to drive her toward that release, knowing she'd been on the edge of it since that morning when everything had changed. Her breath grew short, her movements grew more erratic and her legs shook as she rode him harder and faster.

And she was pulling him right along with her, every thrust sending building pleasure up his length and making him want to fill her to brim with his release.

Peter pushed from the chair and moved toward them. He leaned over from behind the couch and kissed Merritt. She made a muffled moan against his lips and tongue as she flexed even harder.

As Peter pulled away he gripped Elliot's hair, tugging his head back to force him to look at him. "Don't you come, my lord," he growled. "Don't you fucking dare."

Elliot nearly broke that order immediately when Peter dropped his mouth down and kissed him, thrusting his tongue like it was a cock, sucking him like Merritt had a few moments before. Peter released him roughly and stayed exactly where he was as Merritt came apart around Elliot.

She threw her head back as her broken, ragged cries filled the air. The flex of her was maddening, streaking pleasure through his entire body, taunting him with the edge of his own release. And it took every fraction of control he had ever exerted in his life to keep from doing exactly what he had been told not to.

When she flopped forward, her gasping breaths hot against Elliot's lips, Peter moved around the settee. He caught her elbows and gently helped her to her feet. Elliot groaned as her warm, still-twitching body was removed from his hard cock. Peter guided her to the chair where he'd been watching and helped her get situated.

And then he turned on Elliot. And there was no denying what was about to happen. Peter moved to him in a few long steps and then dropped to his knees before him in the same place Merritt had been.

"She made a mess of you, didn't she?" Peter asked, arching a brow in Elliot's direction as he dragged a fingertip along the backside of Elliot's cock, through the wet result of Merritt's orgasm.

"Yes," Elliot gasped in a garbled tone. "Yes."

"Then let me clean you up," Peter whispered before he dropped his head down and stroked the flat of his tongue against Elliot's cock.

Elliot twisted at the powerful sensation of this man's mouth closing over his sensitive cock. Peter had no hesitation—he just took him all the way to the back of his throat, then back until Elliot nearly came free of his lips. But he never released him, just repeated the action over and over.

Elliot lifted into him, matching his rhythm, stars exploding before his eyes as Peter gagged on him and sucked him. Elliot threaded his fingers into the other man's hair, hands shaking as he guided him into a harder, faster rhythm. Peter met it, rocking his own hips as if this excited him.

Elliot was drowning in a haze of sensation and he turned his head, finding Merritt. She was flopped back on the chair, watching them, her hand moving wildly between her legs as her gasping moans merged with theirs. Their eyes met and she nodded.

"Yes," she said. "Yes, yes."

She was urging him on, the refrain fading but her eyes continuing it on. He felt the orgasm he had held back while she fucked him rising back up, more powerful than ever, a wave that could tear him to pieces and he would revel in every one.

"Come!" Merritt shouted, and Elliot looked down. Peter was watching him as he mouth-fucked him, and nodded ever so slightly. Permission granted by this man who had somehow become the master of his pleasure.

Elliot gripped Peter's hair with both hands, arching into him as he roared out his name and poured into his throat. Peter took every single drop, drinking him down like he was the finest wine and only letting his cock loose from his lips when Elliot was fully spent and twitching.

Peter rose to his feet and reached for Merritt without even looking at her. She moved toward him, leaning up to kiss him.

"You taste like Elliot," she whispered, and looked down at the shell of what was left of him.

"And you," Peter corrected. "Now sit on his lap and open your legs."

She turned her back to Elliot and sank down on his lap. His poor cock was too depleted to respond, even though the feeling of her grinding into his lap was absolute bliss. He caught her thighs, draping her legs on the outside of his own, stretching her open for the man who leaned over her and pressed his thick cock into the remaining wetness that Elliot had created earlier.

She whimpered, and Peter caught the sound on his tongue as he began to ravish her willing body. He kissed her again and Merritt wailed against his tongue. She was purely animal now, as lost to sensation and desire as Elliot had been earlier. He reached between their bodies— the bodies of his lovers—and pressed his fingers against her clitoris, urging her toward the edge.

Peter lifted his head and gazed past her, toward Elliot. He leaned in and Elliot met him, driving his tongue into Peter's mouth this time, stroking in time to the other man's long strokes in Merritt's pussy.

Her orgasm was powerful enough that she lifted off Elliot's lap, almost levitating with sensation. Peter swore against Elliot's mouth and grasped her cheek, turning her into their kiss so it was suddenly all three of them and their seeking tongues, their passionate kiss.

Peter grunted and began to move. His release splashed against her stomach, against Elliot's hand, hot and sticky pleasure. Elliot couldn't resist. He lifted his wet fingers, sucking them clean of the salty sweet essence as Peter collapsed on the settee beside him with a resounding, "Fuck."

"I agree," Merritt said weakly, and slithered next to Elliot on the settee. She cuddled against his chest, her hand resting against his heart.

He couldn't respond. He was too stripped down to the bone. By pleasure, by this experience, by the recognition that his world had been changed. For the better, yes. But he would never look at himself in the mirror and be able to pretend away this part of him again.

It was freeing. And slightly terrifying. And he had no idea what it would lead to tomorrow, next week or next year.

CHAPTER 9

Merritt

Never before had Merritt seen Elliot sleep so deeply. Normally the tiniest sound or movement woke him, but this morning he was flat on his stomach, unmoving. She turned on her side toward him, then looked past him to where Peter had fallen asleep after they'd gotten Elliot into bed the previous night.

Her two men. Hers. And each other's now.

On the settee, it had been the first time she'd felt like they truly all made love together. Before it had been powerful, yes. But both men had only been focused on her. Not that she was complaining, of course. To have two such amazing men driven to make her shake with pleasure? She could only be so fortunate.

But on the settee last night, it had been about *all* of them. Pleasure for pleasure, no one person rising above the rest. Everyone fitting into each other and offering a piece of the full puzzle.

She'd wanted more, but Peter had dissuaded her. After such a powerful exchange, they all needed to sort out what had happened. What feelings had been brought up. What realizations had been had by them all.

Peter leaned up on his elbows and smiled at her from across Elliot. "Good morning," he whispered.

She reached across her husband to take Peter's hand in hers, which he lifted to his mouth and kissed gently. A needy fire lit between her legs immediately. God's teeth, she was a wanton. She'd known that for a long while, celebrated it regularly in her marriage bed, but these two men seemed determined to prove it over and over.

He arched a brow like he could read her mind. "Wicked little minx," he whispered.

"Yes," Elliot said without lifting his head or opening his eyes. "She certainly is that. Like a lovely little cat in heat, arching her back and lifting herself to be had."

"You cannot judge me for what you made me, my lord," she teased, and leaned down to kiss the back of his shoulder. He rolled toward her, sliding his fingers through her hair, drawing her down for a more proper kiss. Then he looked to Peter, still a little uncertain.

Peter seemed nothing like it and pressed his own kiss to Elliot's lips. Elliot gave a satisfied sigh as he pulled away.

"The servants come back today," he announced. "To tidy up for us and bring fresh supplies."

Merritt couldn't help the disappointment that moved through her at the idea of an interruption of this dreamworld, even a brief one. "When?"

Elliot sat up partially and squinted at the clock on the mantel. He was utterly adorable with his dark hair mussed and his normally stern face more relaxed. "Er, a couple of hours."

"Well, that gives us all time to dress and ready ourselves and eat," Merritt said. "But then what should we do? I know no one will bother us if we stay in the house, but we can't exactly sit on the settee and diddle each other while they dust around us."

"Or can we?" Peter asked with a wicked waggle of his eyebrows. "Put on a show? I'm very good at writing the script."

She leaned across Elliot and swatted Peter lightly. "No, we cannot. I may not seem like I care, but I make a concerted effort not to scandalize the poor servants!"

Elliot rolled his eyes toward Peter. "She's a terrible prude that way."

A choked laugh was Peter's response. "Yes, I can see that about her. You and I will have to work harder to loosen her up."

"If you loosen me any further, I will be nothing but a pile of orgasming flesh." Merritt arched her brow. "Now stop taunting me long enough to help me come to a decision. What should we do today while the house is occupied?"

"I got up earlier and noted what a gorgeous day it looks to be," Peter said. "What about a long walk together? We haven't exactly been taking advantage of this beautiful setting."

Elliot shook his head. "Oh yes, we have." He reached out to trace his hand down Merritt's side and she shivered. Then he withdrew. "But a walk would likely do us all good."

"And a picnic?" Merritt asked.

Elliot's eyes lit up with pleasure at the idea. "Yes. I know a cove just up the beach that would be the perfect place. Let's get ready and then off we go."

Merritt nodded and began to rise from the bed, but Peter caught her hand and dragged her back, pulling her across Elliot so she was lying half on her husband and half in the slender space between the men.

"Countersuggestion," Peter said with a wicked smile. "First we take turns forcing Merry to make that sound we both like so much."

"Oh, yes," Elliot agreed, his eyes lighting up even further. "*That* sound. I would very much like to hear her make that sound."

"And *then* we can take our walk," Peter said, coaxing his hands down her body. Elliot's joined, their fingers tangling over her with the purpose of her pleasure. Merritt relaxed back and let them worship her, seduce her, let them make her believe this was all that existed and nothing else would ever matter.

Elliot

Sitting on a picnic blanket beside a quiet cove hidden along a long stretch of beach, Elliot couldn't help but watch his wife and Peter interact. He'd been doing it all day, since they'd headed out of the house together after the arrival of the servants. He'd watched them walk at his side, her in the middle, their hands close together. Sometimes her fingers fluttered, like she wished to tangle them with Peter's but something held her back.

Like holding his hand was more intimate or a betrayal in a way that letting Peter eat her pussy while Elliot watched wasn't.

He'd watched them laugh and pick shells and play along the sand. It was like discovering a while new side to Merritt. One she very rarely showed when she was being proper marchioness and mistress of his household. No wonder Peter called her Merry. She was far more that bright emotion when the other man was near her.

A fact Elliot tried to accept rather than sting from. It was not an easy thing to do.

And now he watched as they worked together to gather up the remnants of the picnic they'd all just shared. There was an ease with which they moved and talked. They brought up old stories from their childhood and people they'd known and it was as if no time had ever separated them. Elliot found himself wondering what might have happened if they had never been so cruelly parted as younger people.

What would Merritt's life had been like if she married a man she loved, rather than one she was forced to attach herself to? Peter had mentioned the poverty when the two men discussed that question days before...but what about the rest?

Would she have been happier as Mrs. Reid rather than Lady Egerton?

Elliot stung at the thought, and this time he made no effort to push that feeling away. He couldn't, after all, because his life's work in the last decade had been making his wife happy. Giving her whatever she needed.

Including Peter.

"You suddenly look *very* serious," Merritt said, inching closer to Elliot on the blanket. She reached up to cup her cheek. "Where have you gone?"

He forced a flutter of a smile over his lips. "I was just thinking about the fact that in all the times you and I have gone to the Donville Masquerade to play, we've never seen Peter."

Her eyes went wide. "Well, that is definitely an interesting subject matter. Perhaps Peter doesn't have a membership to Donville."

Both Elliot and Peter burst into laughter at that suggestion. The Donville Masquerade was London's most scandalous hell. A place to game, yes. But also a place for pleasure and sin. Elliot and Merritt had gone many times, to watch the erotic games. And sometimes to participate.

"Of course I have a membership," Peter said when he could manage to speak. "It is *the* place to be for a profligate wanton like myself, my dear."

She pursed her lips at their teasing. "Very well, you needn't mock. Then my husband's observation is actually true. We are regular attendees, so it does seem odd we hadn't met there."

Peter shifted on the blanket and Elliot tilted his head at the sudden discomfort that swept over his face. "Oh, it seems our esteemed Mr. Reid has something to say. A secret he's keeping."

"Can you read me so well, my lord?" Peter asked, meeting his gaze and holding there. "Am I so obvious to you now that you've had my mouth on you?"

Elliot shivered at the tension that now coursed between them. Instant and hot and with only one potential end in sight. One he very much looked forward to now that he'd felt it.

"You were obvious even before your lovely mouth was on me."

"Reading people is what he does," Merritt said softly. "Marking every little shift in breath and expression."

"And *you* benefit from it," Elliot retorted, arching his brow to dare her to deny the truth of what he said.

She smiled slightly. "I never said I didn't."

"What Elliot has made note of, this secret he believes I have," Peter said after a hesitation, "is that I…I *have* seen you two at Donville. More than once."

Elliot exchanged a brief look with Merritt and then together they both stared at Peter.

"I…" she said with a shake of her head. "What do you mean you *saw* us?"

"The first time was a handful of years ago," Peter said, scrubbing a hand through his hair and tousling the blond locks so he now looked a little rakish. "I was there to play. In fact, I was there with a lady. And I looked across the room and there you two were."

Elliot's eyebrows shot up. "You and I knew each other by then—I'd been your patron for years. Why didn't you approach us?"

Peter's eyes went wide. "And do and say what? Say good evening to my former love interest and her husband, who held the keys to my financial position?" He chuckled. "No. I think not."

"Fair enough," Elliot said. "So what *did* you do?"

"Watched you," Peter admitted, and his tone went rough. "Kept out of your sight while you took in the entertainments. While I tracked how Merry touched you, how you couldn't keep your mouth off of her skin. You went into one of the back rooms and I went my own way and had a very good time."

"Can you imagine if you had approached us?" Elliot asked, and shivered. "Joined us back then?"

"Would you have been ready for such a thing?" Peter asked. "I think you hated me a little back then."

"Hated him?" Merritt repeated, and looked at Elliot. "Did you hate Peter even though you were his patron?"

He tilted his head. "Not hated," he said softly. Only what he'd felt back then was very similar to hate. Jealousy. So perhaps Peter was correct that he wouldn't have been ready to welcome the other man into their bed.

To share Merritt. To share himself.

"So you saw us at the hell," Elliot said, clearing his throat. "That isn't much of a secret, my friend."

Peter lifted his brows. "I wasn't finished. I saw you again, many times, after that. I always kept myself in the shadows, watching. Until one night, about a year ago, when I followed you to the back."

Elliot straightened up. The Donville Masquerade's back rooms were made for assignations, passionate joinings. But they were also built for those who wished to watch and be watched. There were little doors on panels in the wall of each chamber. If they were left open, someone in the passageway behind could watch.

And Merritt had always liked being watched.

"You stood in the passageway and observed us?" she whispered.

"I watched you fuck," Peter corrected gently. "Watched you move together like you'd been built to do so, watched you come, Merry, until the tears were streaming down your face. Watched him fill you up and then start all over again. I watched you and I pleasured myself. And I fantasized about it over and over again until that moment when all…almost all of the fantasies came true."

Merritt and Elliot were each stock-still a moment, then Merritt crawled across the blanket and cupped Peter's cheeks. She pressed her mouth to his, licking and stroking and teasing until his arms came around her waist and he tugged her flat against his chest.

Only then did she pull away and smile up at him. "That makes me wild, you know. Knowing you were watching us." She glanced back at Elliot. "I know it drives *you* wild."

Elliot kept his gaze on Peter. His wife was not wrong that the idea that Peter had watched them together was arousing beyond measure. But he had other thoughts, as well. "You said *almost* every fantasy. What did you picture in that wicked mind of yours as you stroked your cock and thought of us?"

Now Peter pushed away from Merritt and eased his way across the blanket toward Elliot. When he reached him, he pressed a hand into his thigh. He leaned in but didn't allow Elliot his mouth. He teased his lips along Elliot's jaw, just brushing there, never enough pressure.

"I used to imagine you fucking me like you fucked her," he murmured. "While I did the same to her. You stretching me with that wonderful cock, Elliot. *That's* what I pictured."

He drew back then and Merritt made a ragged sigh from behind them.

Elliot swallowed. This was the next step to all of this. Penetrating this man and his cock twitched at the thought of taking him.

"You didn't imagine taking me?" he whispered, speaking out loud the thing he wanted.

Peter smirked. "Oh yes. I definitely pictured myself perched behind you, using that arse while I stroked you to completion and she fingered herself. But you, my lord, are the only one of the three of us who hasn't already engaged in arseplay. Or am I wrong?"

"You are not wrong," Elliot managed to whisper. *Whimper*.

"So you must be readied so that it will be a pleasure, not a pain," Peter said. "In the meantime, would you like to fuck me?"

As he said it, he cupped Elliot's cock through his trousers. He was rock hard, he knew it, and it was the answer he managed to choke out. "Yes."

Peter kissed him at last, his tongue stroking and thrusting the way Elliot would soon do to him, with his cock. Then he pulled away and got up, offering first a hand to help Merritt and then Elliot.

"Then I suggest we go back. Because I cannot wait one more moment."

CHAPTER 10

Merritt

The cottage was empty as they entered it, but it was obvious the servants had done their duties. Every room was spotless. Even the bannisters shone as Merritt followed Elliot up the stairs, Peter trailing behind her, his hand on her lower back.

She was shaking with thoughts of what was about to happen. She was going to watch as her husband took Peter. She was going to feel them all move together in a new and wonderful way as they unlocked Elliot's desires one by one.

After so many years of him tending hers, she was thrilled to be a part of the same for him.

They entered the bedroom. The bed had been turned and remade and she laughed because it seemed like a lot of effort for the three of them to just make a mess of everything again.

A glorious, gorgeous mess.

Peter had no sooner closed the door behind himself than Elliot came to them. He cupped the back of Merritt's neck, drawing her to him to kiss her, then switched to kissing Peter. She began to unbutton his shirt as they dove into each other, revealing inch by inch of Elliot's glorious body.

Even after a decade, she was still moved by him. Still aroused when he tugged his shirt over his head and went right back to kissing Peter. She leaned forward, dragging her tongue along his chest, sucking one flat nipple hard enough that he gasped against Peter's mouth.

He dug his fingers into her loosely bound hair and tilted her head up, crushing his mouth to hers, then turning her face so Peter could do the same. She raked her nails across Elliot's chest lightly as Peter slid her between them and they both rocked into her, Peter from behind, Elliot against the front.

Their mouths moved over her, Peter's against the side of her throat, Elliot's against her lips. Hands slid against her body and she wasn't even sure whose were whose after a few moments. It was intoxicating and she never wanted it to end.

But she managed to come up from the hum of her own pleasure and look at Elliot. She wanted so much to give pleasure to him. She wanted to give him everything he'd ever desired and suppressed. So she unfastened his fall front and slowly slid his trousers down his hips.

He stared down at her, groaning as she took him in hand and stroked. Peter reached around her, his fingers tangling with hers, and together they pulled at him, working him as his eyes fluttered shut and he pushed against their combined hands.

"You know," she whispered, licking the column of his throat lightly. "The way you readied me for you in my arse was through the toys. Which are clean, and could be ready for you while you have Peter."

Elliot's eyes came open, wide and wild at the suggestion. He glanced at her, then Peter. "Yes," he finally hissed out.

She smiled and moved to the table beside the bed. She withdrew the velvet bag with the toy and the bottle of oil he'd placed there for her pleasure. When she turned back she found that Peter had removed his shirt. She stared as Elliot rubbed his hands over the other man's chest, as Peter continued to tug the marquess's cock gently.

"Take them off," Elliot grunted, and motioned to Peter's trousers.

Peter gave a half-smile and did as he'd been told. Now both men were naked. She was the only one clothed. There was something wicked about that. Peter leaned back against the edge of the bed and Elliot drew in a deep breath before he bent over and lightly licked Peter's cock.

As he did so, hesitant at first, but gaining more certainty as Peter dug his fingers into his hair and groaned, Merritt stepped up behind her husband. She stroked her hands over his backside, kneading the muscle there. He spread his legs a little wider, offering himself to her. When she began to spread the oil over his arse, he stopped sucking Peter and looked over his shoulder at her.

His pupils were huge with desire and he looked so wicked, so utterly beautiful that it took everything in her not to just wedge herself between them and demand that Elliot fuck her to oblivion.

Instead, she focused on slowly easing the plug into his body. He tensed a little as she did so, and she smiled. "Relax."

He drew a breath and the toy moved, seated fully into him. His cock got even harder and he went back to licking Peter's with even more abandon.

"Here," Peter said, taking her hand and moving her between them. "Fuck your wife."

Merritt shivered as Peter stepped away and Elliot caught her waist, lifting her on the bed, pushing her back. He shoved her skirts up and stroked her sex with the flat of his hand. He leaned in and spread her wider. His gaze held hers as he spit on her, making her even wetter as he massaged his fingers into her.

Then he drove forward and his cock slid home.

She lifted into him as he pumped slowly once, twice, three times, coating his cock with her excitement. He murmured her name, a desperate plea as Peter pressed a hand to Elliot's chest and gently eased him away. She whimpered at the loss of him filling her, but the disappointment faded as Peter handed the discarded bottle of oil to Elliot and then turned back to her.

"So pretty," he whispered. "You are so pretty spread out for me, Merry. Good enough to eat."

She pressed a hand to the back of his head and pushed him toward her. "Then do it."

He chuckled low and heated, and then he did just that, burying his face between her thighs and drawing his tongue across her entrance. He began to moan against her as he tongued her, pleasure from tasting her mixed with the pleasure as Elliot began to ready him.

She watched as her husband focused on that task with the same care he always focused on her. And there was the tiniest flare of jealousy mixed with the arousal at the realization that Elliot wanted Peter the same way he did her.

Elliot lifted his gaze and caught hers, holding there as he stepped back to let her watch as he stroked oil down the thick, hard length of his cock. He moved against Peter and positioned himself.

She shivered against Peter's tongue as he began focus on her clitoris. And she shivered because of how Elliot closed his eyes in pure bliss as he began to enter Peter.

The three of them moaned in unison, their pleasure so tangled now that it was all part of the same origin. She rolled against Peter's tongue, he pushed against Elliot's cock, Elliot gripped Peter's hips as he took until he was fully seated. She knew what he felt like inside and reveled in Peter's soft sigh of pleasure that vibrated against her aching clitoris.

Elliot stroked once, slow and gentle, and Peter lifted his head with a curse. Elliot smiled and leaned over him, even as he watched Merritt.

"Fuck her," he ordered, all a man in control again.

She bucked as Peter sucked her clitoris hard one more time,

drawing her right to the edge of release. Then he lifted his head and whispered, "Oh, with great pleasure."

~

Elliot

The clench of Peter's body around Elliot's cock was almost enough to unman him and he was only on the first of many strokes. He drew in a long breath, trying to control himself. An almost impossible task considering the scene before him.

Elliot lifted his head from Merritt's pussy and set a hand on either side of her head. He shifted, bringing Elliot with him, rubbing his cock against her entrance as she writhed.

She was so close to the edge. It would take nothing to bring her over. Elliot loved to watch it, loved to see her nipples pucker and skin flush with pleasure, loved to see her lift her hips in offering as Peter took her.

And now they were all bound in a different way. Their pleasure linked. Together he and Peter began to move, their hips flexing in time. He fucked Peter, Peter fucked Merritt, she stroked her fingers over her clitoris as she lifted and moaned as she stared at the two of them.

When he sped up, Peter followed suit. When he ground his hips, Peter's harsh cries and the flex of his hips was the reward. For a moment Elliot felt the rush of this wonderful thing. Watching Peter fuck his wife, all while he controlled Peter's movements like a puppet master, was so arousing he once again fought not to spend.

And yet that was exactly what all of them were racing toward. Merritt had already begun to shake, her thighs trembling as she gripped them tighter around Peter's hips. Peter was sawing back and forth, tugging Elliot's aching cock with every forward thrust into Merritt's slick body.

Pleasure mounted, all new and yet the same. Elliot shut his eyes and fell into the warmth of it, drowning in sensation as Peter clenched at him, as he pushed through the tightness and heat, as he heard Merritt shout as she came.

The pleasure overtook him as he opened his eyes to watch her writhe on the coverlet, her expression twisted with sensation. Watching her come had always pushed him over the edge. Combined with the feel of Peter around him, it was too much. He gripped the other man's hips and pounded all the harder. Peter met him stroke for stroke, and then together they barked out release. Peter withdrew from Merritt and came, Elliot let himself pump inside Peter. And they all collapsed in a pile or arms and legs, sweat and come, passion and relief at last.

He leaned in, his tongue finding both of theirs at once, tasting their combined flavors as he slowly withdrew from Peter and they shifted into a curled mass of limbs and bodies.

For years Elliot had secretly fantasized about an experience like this. And now that he'd had it, he realized he hadn't even been close to the kind of pleasure he'd just felt. A pleasure bound by emotion, by connection...a pleasure he worried would soon be lost because their week was more than halfway over.

And then he had no idea what would happen.

CHAPTER 11

Peter

Another morning broke, soft light from the curtains they had left open the night before hitting Peter's face and forcing him from exhausted, sated slumber. He opened one eye and looked around him. Merritt was no longer in the bed, but Elliot was there, his dark head resting against Peter's stomach, the marquess's arm tucked around Peter's hip.

Peter smiled and reached down to thread his fingers through the thick mass of Elliot's hair. As a response, Elliot grunted and cuddled a bit closer.

"That's nice," he murmured without opening his eyes.

"I agree," Peter said, and sucked in a breath as Elliot turned his mouth against his stomach and kissed him there gently. "You are too good at that," he said, a little more raggedly as Elliot's fingers began to stroke against his hip.

"Too good at what?" Elliot asked, his voice muffled as he kissed Peter's skin again, his breath hot.

"Finding every little spot for pleasure and then tormenting a person with them," Peter said, tugging Elliot's hair to tilt his face up.

The marquess stared up at him, dark eyes dilated with desire. "I see you do it with Merry, too. Always finding the way to please everyone around you."

"Only those I…" Elliot's brow wrinkled and he cut himself off. "What is your point, Peter. Do you want me to stop?"

"No," Peter said. "Not at all. I just wonder if you ever truly let anyone else in far enough to do the same for you."

There was a moment when Peter knew his question hit Elliot in the chest. He saw the flare of panic in the other man's eyes, swiftly followed by anger. Elliot sat up, pulling from Peter's arms, breaking the lazy, sensual pleasure of the morning.

"What do you care?" he asked sharply.

Peter examined him, seeing the walls come up between them. The ones that hadn't actually ever been fully knocked down. Elliot gave his body, yes. Or more to the point, gave everything so that Peter and Merry were satisfied. But when it came to who he was, what he felt, Peter wasn't certain either of them had really ever known that. He felt Merry's frustration about that fact from time to time. Felt her lean toward her husband with an edge of desperation.

And he understood it so much more now.

"Because I want to see you have some tiny fraction of what you give," he said gently.

"I get plenty," Elliot protested. "I haven't complained."

"No, I don't think you ever would." Peter shook his head. "Maybe you should."

"I grew up with a man who complained and took and didn't give a fuck about anyone else but himself." Elliot glared at him. "And you won't convince me to be like him, not for your pleasure."

And there it was in one broken expression. Peter understood Elliot on a level he never had before.

"Does Merry know?" he asked after a beat had passed.

Elliot sighed. "Yes. She knew my father. She saw what our relationship was like. She comforted me when he was dead and all I had left was the pain he caused in his wake."

"Good," Peter said softly. "At least you let her do that."

Elliot lay back on the pillows, not touching Peter, and stared up at the ceiling. "It wasn't easy. I'm not like you two. I can't just…spill myself out for others to see. He…he punished me for that. And I learned very young not to ask for too much. To prove myself worthy of attention or praise or…"

He trailed off and Peter reached out to rest his hand on Elliot's naked chest. He could feel the other man's heart beating hard against his fingers. The only indication he gave of how difficult this was because he had been trained to hide emotions that might be construed as…messy. Uncomfortable for someone else.

"Or love?" Peter suggested.

"Love was for the weak," Elliot whispered, and his voice broke just a fraction. "Wanting love was for the weak."

Peter leaned on his side and scooted next to him, close enough that their bodies touched again. He cupped Elliot's cheek and turned his face into his. "I'm sorry," he murmured. "I'm sorry he told you that lie and that you believed it."

Then he bent his head and took Elliot's mouth gently, hoping he would allow Peter to give to him. Just give. Before this was over and it might be too late.

Elliot

It wasn't that no one had ever talked to Elliot about his father. He and Merritt had discussed the late marquess often, especially when the old man had died. She had held Elliot, soothed him, given him all the warmth and care in the world so he could collapse. And he had, just once. It had terrified him to let her see him in that state and he had vowed never to do it again.

But here he was, Peter leaning over him, holding him steady on the bed, kissing him. And he wanted so, so much, to just…let him. To relax his death grip on control like he had the first time Peter had taken him into his mouth…only let it last more than a few moments. To really give himself to this man. And to Merritt. To be weak, if only for them.

Peter's mouth dragged lower, away from his lips, across his jawline, down the side of his throat. He lifted into the sensations of the other man's touch, closing his eyes so he could just…feel. Peter's lips latched around his nipple, sucking until he reached the very edge of pain. He set his hand on the back of Peter's head, but Peter shook it as he reached up to pin Elliot's hands to the bed.

"Just for you," he whispered. "Let this be just for you."

Elliot stared at him, knowing he could refuse. Knowing he could break Peter's firm hold on his wrists if he wanted to. Refuse to allow him to do this.

"Don't you want it to be just for him, Merry?" Peter asked, keeping his stare locked with Elliot's.

Elliot turned his face and found Merritt in the doorway, a tray in her hands. She was staring at them, mouth partly agape, desire and emotion all over her lovely face. But Peter's question seemed to jolt her to action.

"Oh yes," she murmured as she entered the room and set the tray of food on the table by the fire. She practically glided toward the bed, hands trembling as she joined them. Peter kept holding him down, gentle but firm as she settled in beside Elliot, cupped his face and kissed him deeply.

"Merritt," he managed to moan around her tongue. When she pulled away, he stared up into her face, uncertain what to say or do in this situation.

"Please let us," she whispered back. "Let us."

It was her request that forced the ultimate surrender. After all, he could never deny her. So he nodded and tugged his hands from Peter's. But instead of reaching for his two remarkable lovers, as he so desperately wished to do, he placed them behind his head, trapping them against the pillows as he watched Merritt and Peter kiss over his prone body.

They didn't linger on each other long, though. Together, they kissed a trail down his body. It was fire and pleasure, Merritt's hands soft on his skin, Peter more firm and determined as he traced the lines of Elliot's chest and hips and thighs.

At last they each settled with their faces at his hips. His cock was already hard from everything that had come before, and Merritt smiled, as if giving her permission to Peter to begin. He did so, licking a slow circle around the ridiculously sensitive head of Elliot's cock. He jolted with a moan and lifted against Peter's tongue. Merritt laughed, her voice husky in the quiet. She rested a hand on his hip to hold him steady and then bent her head. She sucked the shaft of his cock, then lower to trace her tongue over his balls.

He couldn't breathe as the pleasure spiked between them. First they teased him, just licking and tasting, tormenting with tongues and fingers. Kissing each other as often as they licked him. But soon they both grew more focused. They took turns with him, taking his cock in their mouths, sucking him. Building him toward release. And he ached for it as the need grew, making his balls heavy, streaking pleasure up his length.

"Please," he murmured at last. "I want…"

"You want to come," Peter said. "That's all you need to do, Elliot. All we want. You come for us."

Elliot glanced at Merritt, who guided his cock to her lips as Peter spoke. She nodded, holding his stare as she sucked him. He groaned as she took him, as Peter stroked the length she couldn't manage in her throat. It was almost the point of no return. The place where he would do exactly as they desired, exactly as he feared: he would let go. He would hand himself over, never giving anything in return.

And he would take instead of earning.

"Please," Peter whispered. The strong fingers of one hand

worked the base of Elliot's cock as the other traced his jawline. "Please."

Elliot couldn't deny them, or himself, any longer. He came with a roar. Merritt pulled away, his come splashing on her cheeks. Peter opened his mouth, and together they each let him come against their tongues as he groaned in pure pleasure. At last Peter and Merritt kissed, each moaning in desire and pleasure of their own.

But they didn't do anything more. Slowly they each took their place next to him, arms embracing him, holding him as if they would each protect him. Protect *him*. These two people he had worshipped and pleasured and taken care of for years…they were offering him something so precious now in return.

But he frowned even as the pleasure faded slowly. They offered him everything in this cottage, for a short time. But would that offer extend beyond this week of pleasure and bliss? Because it was hard for him to imagine that he could truly surrender to them after they returned to London. Surrender himself to two people who had loved each other first, long before either had known him. Surrender himself without doing anything else in return except be himself.

That…well, that seemed like the real fantasy of this place. And he wasn't certain it was one he could live when these heady days were over.

CHAPTER 12

Peter

Peter scrubbed a hand through his hair as he entered the kitchen one late afternoon a few days later. He found Elliot there, just as he had expected, brewing tea for a very late breakfast that the marquess had already arranged on a tray.

"I wondered where you'd gone," Peter said as he crossed to kiss Elliot.

Elliot softened to the caress, but then went back to his work. "I said I was going to gather breakfast."

There was something sharp in his tone and Peter tilted his head at it. "Well, I've come to help."

"I don't need help." Elliot turned to the kettle and poured hot water into the teapot.

Peter stared at him. Since the morning he and Merry had sucked Elliot's cock together, when he had surrendered fully to them for perhaps the first time, Elliot had been softer. More open. But now he was back to being the harder, harsher marquess. And Peter didn't understand why.

"What is wrong with you?" he asked. "Did I...do something to offend you?"

"No." Elliot's tone was gentler, but he didn't look up from the small adjustments he was making to the tray. "No. I suppose I'm just thinking about what comes next. Already in my head about the trip home tomorrow."

Peter lifted his brows. "I haven't thought that far ahead, but I suppose it is a good question to ask. What...what does happen tomorrow?"

Now Elliot did look at him, dark eyes lifting, moving over his face, hesitating on his lips, then drifting away. Desire and tension, almost like they'd gone back to the beginning. Peter found himself wanting to grasp at keeping Elliot here instead.

"Merritt and I will go home," Elliot said softly. "And I suppose you will soon follow, as I know you are putting on your next play very soon. There must be much to do."

"I wasn't talking about plays, Elliot," Peter said, and grabbed for his hand.

Elliot stared at their intertwined digits for a moment, flexing his fingers in Peter's. Then he slowly drew himself away. "I don't know," he admitted. "Everything has changed, hasn't it? Especially in the last few days. And I will confess that I am not certain about what that means for me. For you, for her."

"What about for *us*?" Peter asked. "Isn't this a discussion for us, since it is about us?" Elliot huffed out a breath and Peter wrinkled his brow. "You aren't going lord of the manor on me about this, are you? Deciding you know best for all of us? I thought we had moved past that."

"I don't know best about anything," Elliot snapped. "I'm wondering if I ever did." He ran a hand through his hair and shook his head. "Look, I apologize. I'm in an ill humor thinking about everything that needs to be done before we go home. Why don't I just go into Brighton, make the arrangements, and I'll try to be in a better mindset when I return?"

Peter drew in a breath. He could understand where Elliot was coming from, in truth. The marquess was a serious person, one who had spent a lifetime holding back some part of himself. The last few days of utter surrender and vulnerability were likely not easy for him.

"Very well," he said as gently as he could. "I'll take the tray to Merry and explain. And we'll be waiting for you when you return."

Elliot stared at the tray he'd made and then up at Peter. "Yes. Fine. Thank you."

He said nothing else, he made no effort to touch Peter. He just turned and left the kitchen. Leaving Peter entirely confused and worried about what exactly Elliot's ill humor meant.

Merritt

Merritt sat curled up in the big bed, covers wrapped around her and a book dangling unread from her fingertips. How could she concentrate on anything after the last few days? Since the first time Elliot had taken Peter, there had only been building pleasure between them all. They shared in her and each other, and together Peter and Merritt trained Elliot so that he would be ready for Peter's cock. They watched each other, they learned each other, and the power of all of it only seemed to grow.

But as their time together was beginning to wane—Merritt and Elliot were meant to return to London the next day—more questions were being raised than answers. Only none of them had posed those questions yet. None of them had dared to raise their hand and say they wanted more. Because how? How could it work?

She could feel Elliot's reaction to the truth. He'd begun to withdraw the morning. He'd left the bed first, saying he was going to make breakfast. When he hadn't returned in a reasonable time, Merritt had known he was in an ill humor. Brooding. Peter had gone after him and she had decided to pretend to read so she wouldn't fret.

Reality felt like it was creeping into her fantasy. And it was all too soon.

"Merry?"

She looked up to find Peter standing in the chamber entryway, an overladen tray in his hands. She smiled at him and got up to help as he set the tray on the table. She wrapped a robe around herself and looked at the wide variety of options laid out before her.

"He does think of everything. Down to the way he places a flower along the edge of my plate." She looked behind Peter, but Elliot didn't appear. Her heart sank. "He…he left?"

Peter glanced down at her. "How did you know?"

"That faraway look in his eyes this morning. He's already starting to count the hoof falls back to London." She shook her head.

"He was…angry, I think," Peter said softly.

She pursed her lips. It seemed she was not alone in her observation of Elliot. "He wasn't angry," she said. "When he is angry, you don't have to question. He's…withdrawing."

"Because this week is coming to an end."

She nodded. "He'll distance himself. He'll try to make himself believe that it didn't mean anything. But I know him after all this time. I know it meant *everything*."

"It did to me," Peter said. He looked at her for a long, charged moment and there was something that lit in his stare. Not desire. Well, not only desire, for that was always there when he looked at her. Something…deeper.

He took her hand and threaded their fingers together. "I have to say something, even though I perhaps shouldn't. But I already know regret when it comes to you and I won't live through it again."

"What is it?" she asked, even though she knew. She knew what he would say.

"I still love you, Merritt," he said.

It was so matter of fact. So easy for him to confess those wonderful and painful words. She blinked at the tears that stung her eyes and nodded. "And I still love you, too."

Peter's expression softened. He cupped her face and leaned in to kiss her. She opened to him, gripping his wrist with one hand, placing the other on his chest. Together they sighed, this physical connection different than any they had shared in the past week… different because they had finally said those words that had hung between them for what felt like a lifetime.

He wrapped an arm around her waist and drew her closer, even as he backed her toward the bed. She threaded her fingers through his hair and lifted into him, as if she could get close enough that they wouldn't be parted again.

Perhaps they would have made love then, tangled together on the bed, love pulsing between them with as much power as desire. But before they could go so far, Merritt looked up and gasped.

Elliot was standing in the doorway, watching them. And not watching them with desire, like he had every other time he'd seen them so involved with each other. Not even watching them with the jealousy that sometimes flared in his expression when they touched.

No, he was watching them with an expression of…*devastation.* Hurt. Betrayal.

She pushed away from Peter, and he looked over his shoulder to see the same thing she did. They rose together, each smoothing their clothing like it could erase how they'd become wrinkled.

"Elliot," Merritt whispered, and moved toward him.

He shook his head but said nothing. He just backed from the room and closed the door behind himself. She stared, gape-mouthed, at the barrier he had put between them. At the pain she had felt coursing from him like waves.

She had hurt him. And she hated herself for it. She bent her head and whispered, "Oh God." She turned toward Peter. "We must talk to him."

Peter's mouth pursed and he slowly shook his head. He looked as sick as she felt. "Not we," he said.

"What?" she gasped. "After everything we've done together, been to each other this past week, you do not think this is a problem for *us* to handle?"

He sighed. "No, I don't. Because he doesn't want to talk to me, Merry. It's complicated."

"It's complicated," she repeated with a snort. "What I just saw was as simple as anything. He saw us together…without him. And he was left out and—"

"You know it's more than that," Peter interrupted. "You know it. That man may want me. He may even care for me more than he ever thought he'd allow himself to do. But he loves *you*. And he fears that I threaten everything in his life that has meaning."

She blinked as she stared at Peter, his words sinking in. She sat back down hard on the bed's edge and shook her head. "Elliot and I have been married for ten years…he's never told me he loves me."

Peter was quiet a moment. "We are very different men. If you had been mine, all those years ago, I would have told you every day. I would have written sonnets. I would have penned plays. I would have found word after word and sentence after sentence to draw it out for you." He motioned toward the door. "*He* is a man of action, not words. It's why he puts a flower on your breakfast tray. Why a marquess fills a tub with hot water until he's slick with sweat from the exertion. Why he brought your former lover here so you could have something that was stolen from you."

Her breath hitched, stolen by the beautiful hope those words created.

Peter continued, "And that's just a small selection of the actions of love I've seen Elliot show you since I've been here. I'm sure over those same ten years that were robbed from us, he's done a thousand other things to reveal how much he loves you. Hasn't he?"

She shivered as a world of memories flooded her. Moments of tenderness and support, moments of passion, times when Elliot had proven he could be trusted, gifts of all kinds that he'd showered over her. Acts of adoration and passion, not just for her body, but for her soul.

She covered her face with her hands. "Yes. Yes, he has shown me that he loves me, perhaps more than I have ever shown him."

Peter touched her chin and tilted it toward him. His green eyes were so sad. "Somehow I doubt that, Merry." He pushed to his feet. "I can't hurt him. And I sure as hell don't want to hurt you. Looking at his face a moment ago, I've failed at avoiding both those things. So I...I should leave."

She caught her breath. "No!" she burst out.

"Yes," he insisted. "Merry, you know it's true. You and Elliot have to work out your lives, your relationship. And once you do...then perhaps we can talk about something more. But only if it's right for both of you." He glanced toward the door. "And I fear it might not ever be that."

She bent her head, tears stinging her eyes, because she knew he was right in what had to happen. And because she feared he might be right about the future.

He cupped her chin and lifted it, brushing his lips to hers. "I will never regret this. And if he can hear it, I hope you'll tell him the same."

"I will," she promised, wiping at the tears that were now falling down her cheeks. He smoothed them away with his thumbs and kissed her again, this time more deeply.

Then he stepped away. Turned away. And left her alone in the room, alone with her thoughts and alone with the realization of what she would have to do to fix all of this.

If she could.

Elliot

Elliot stumbled up the winding, sandy path that led to the cottage in the distance. He'd taken a long walk on the beach, not that he could have told anyone who asked about the beauty of the scenery. His hair was damp, so it must have rained, or he'd been hit by sea spray.

He recalled none of it.

Because his mind kept taking him, over and over, back to the moment when he'd walked into the bedroom to apologize to Peter and Merritt for his ill humor and found them in each other's arms. His ears rang as they replayed their mutual declarations of unending love for each other.

And he'd known what they said was true, even before their overheard confessions. He wasn't blind—he'd felt their connection from the very beginning. He'd nurtured it, for Christ's sake, telling himself it would change nothing. That it would bring Merritt happiness to purge herself from what she had lost and might regret.

But to hear them say those words, so tangled in each other that they didn't even hear the door open, that they didn't see him…that had torn him to shreds.

He'd brought Peter in as a third to their marriage. And for a few beautiful moments he'd thought that relationship between them was equal. That they all had a part to play. But it turned out his greatest fear was true: *he* was the third to a love that had never stopped.

Worse, he hadn't just thought of that moment, playing over in slow motion through his addled mind. But his mind whispered what he had to do about it. What he had to do to make Merritt happy.

He stepped into the foyer, and immediately Merritt came rushing from the parlor where she'd apparently been waiting for him. She was dressed now, her hair pulled back loosely, her face lined with worry as she came to him and threw her arms around him. She was trembling as she clenched her hands along his shoulders and back.

"My God, I was worried sick," she breathed. "Elliot, you've been gone over an hour."

"Was it an hour?" he asked, pulling away from her even though he still felt the ghost of her warmth on his skin. How long would he feel it? Would it haunt him in the night, tingling like a phantom limb?

"Yes." She took his hand and drew him into the parlor.

He looked around. Peter was not there. "Is he upstairs?" he asked, not clarifying who *he* was. There was only one *he* now. "Will you get him? I need to say something to you both."

Merritt shook her head and tears flashed to her eyes. "He…he is gone, Elliot. He's not here."

He stared at her, stunned by how his heart felt as torn by Peter's absence as it had by finding him with Merritt earlier. "What?" he asked. "Gone? He left you?"

She tilted her head. "Not just me, Elliot. You know that in your heart. He left *us*."

CHAPTER 13

Merritt

Elliot's face was blank. He had always been an expert at that: wiping his emotions clear when they became too much for him. When they made him too vulnerable to others…even her. The past few days he'd done it less and she'd hoped…but now he was hard again. Putting up walls between them. Ones she might deserve.

"This is…this is my fault," he said at last, and she heard what he concealed in the slight waver to his voice.

She shook her head. "No. It's not."

"It is," he said, his tone sharper as he paced away from her to the window, staring out intently like he could somehow find Peter and draw him back. "I kept you from him. Not on purpose at first. But now…now I know you love him. And he loves you. If I stand in the way…"

She caught her breath and rushed to him, turning him back to her. She grabbed his hands and clutched them against her chest. "You are not in the way."

His expression softened, filled with pain and certainty. "Of course I am, Merritt. And what I came back to tell you, to tell you both…is that I…" Every word seemed a struggle and he fought it valiantly. "I would let you go."

She was struck silent by that simple sentence. It was like someone had plunged a sword into her heart, into her soul.

"You have given me my heirs and spares," he whispered. "You have given me ten years, wonderful years. So if it would make you happy, I would let you go to him without a fight. With a fine enough settlement that neither of you would never want for anything."

She nearly went to her knees but fought to stay upright. This selfless act was exactly what Peter had been talking about when he spoke of Elliot's numerous acts of love. She saw how much this tore him apart. What he didn't know was how it did the same to her. The idea of losing him? It made all her love for him so very sharp and clear. Because she couldn't picture, not for one moment, a world where they were parted and she was also happy.

"You two men," she said with a shake of her head. "Each so eager to let me go in some effort to give me happiness. And that is *not* what I want, Elliot."

He didn't look certain. "Merritt," he began.

She held up a hand. "When Peter was taken from me all those years ago, it did leave a hole in my heart that was never fully healed or filled."

He flinched but didn't turn away.

"I know that fact hurts you, Elliot, and I cannot express how sorry I am about it. But I also cannot lie."

"I would never expect you to," he whispered.

"But I need you to know something else," she said as she stepped closer. As she cupped his cheeks and smoothed her fingers along the angles there. "*I love my husband.* I *love* you, Elliot."

Elliot

Elliot buckled at those words, the ones he had longed to hear for years but had never pressed for. Words that had burned in his dreams and his fantasies. She wrapped her arms around him, holding him close as unexpected tears welled in his eyes. Emotions he had always tried to suppress overflowed through him, alongside a relief unlike any he'd ever felt. She supported him as he struggled to breathe. To understand what she was saying and accept it. The acceptance was the hardest part.

He didn't want this to be because of pity. Or obligation.

"You—you don't have to say that," he finally managed to choke out.

She tilted her head. "I say it because I mean it."

She drew him to the settee and together they sat, her hands clenching his. Her gaze never wavering. And in it, he found the kernel of hope that he'd never dared reach for.

"I didn't choose my path to you," she said. "I was forced to it. And yes, at the beginning you seemed the best option of the bad lot my father demanded I consider."

"I know that," he murmured.

"But I wouldn't change a step I have taken along this road," she said. "I need you to understand that. If I could go back in time, if I could have everything I desired, I would let Peter be taken from me, and I would choose you. Over and over."

He stared, his ears ringing, his limbs numb. "I-I don't understand."

She smiled. The most beautiful smile that had ever existed in this world. The smile he adored to distraction every time she gifted it in his direction.

"Yes, I loved him. I love him." She shook her head. "But his path has led him to a successful career, a confidence he certainly didn't have as a boy, a life that has made him happy. And my path has brought me three children, who I am proud of and care for. It's brought me pleasure and laughter and friends and *you*. Most of all it's brought me you, Elliot. You are my heart, my soul. I could never and would never give you up."

Her words were becoming clearer, striking through the stunned fog, opening his heart in a way he'd never thought was possible. Breaking him wide open until all there was joy and certainty and happiness unlike anything he'd ever felt before.

He drew her in and kissed her, and it was like the first time. And in a way, he supposed it was. Because loving her and being loved by her would open a new chapter for them. No matter what else needed to be resolved, that was absolutely certain.

She shifted over him, straddling his lap, tightening her arms around him as their kiss slowed and deepened. He sank into the sensation of her mouth, of her hands as they smoothed around his back, over his shoulders, across his chest. He shivered as she sucked his tongue gently and the tenor of their connection shifted to the desire that had always come so deep and easy over the years.

"I want you," she murmured against his mouth. "Please."

He nodded because he could do nothing else. God knew he'd always been weak to her. Together they unbuttoned each other, shifting only to lift clothing away, only to remove boots and stockings. They came back together in the same position at last, naked emotionally and physically.

She drew back, holding his gaze as they aligned their bodies. As she eased down over him and took him in little by little, stroke by stroke, until he was hers. Truly hers.

"Elliot," she whispered, and took his mouth. "I love you," she said against his tongue.

He moved beneath her, she rolled over him and then it was all physical sensation. A slow building toward pleasure and release and vows they said with their bodies every time they made love. Truly made love.

He gripped her hips, guiding her as she ground against him, her breath coming short as her pleasure mounted. When her legs began to shake and grip harder around his thighs, he pulled from her mouth and watched her. He loved watching her come, loved every expression of her pleasure. He drank them in now as she dropped her head back and jerked harder against him. Riding him faster, her body milking him, sending sensation up his cock and through his body.

She was groaning his name over and over now, her fingers digging into his back as she brought him to the brink. And then he fell, lifting into her flexing sheath, pumping her full of himself as he brought her mouth back to his and kissed her again.

He lay back on the settee and she adjusted herself so she was lying on top on him, her legs tangled in his, her hand tracing his jawline as she smiled up at him.

He wrinkled his brow. "You…you know I love you, too, don't you?" he asked. "I realized I didn't say it."

She surprised him by laughing, by pushing up to kiss the very tip of his nose. "Oh yes, I know. I was afraid to believe it, honestly. But…but Peter helped me see it before he left."

"Peter," he repeated, all but tasting the other man on his lips when he said his name.

"Oh, Peter," Merritt said. "What in the world will we do about Peter?"

Elliot stared up at the ceiling and played out a dozen times with the other man. And not just moments they'd shared during this stolen week together, but before. Moments where he'd met Peter's stare in a club and felt the same thrill in his chest that he felt when he met Merritt's across a ballroom.

Moments when Peter's enthusiasm about a play or a piece of art had coaxed a smile from Elliot's lips.

The jealousy and heartbreak that had always gone along with his interactions with Peter, that tickled the back of his mind when he saw Merritt and Peter together, were…gone. He realized that now. Realized they had always existed not because Merritt loved the other man. It was always because he had believed she didn't love *him*.

And now that he knew she did, there was more than enough room for her feelings for Peter. And for his own. The shadow over everything between the three of them was gone. Now that it was, he knew exactly what he wanted to do. What he had to do.

He sat up, forcing Merritt to do the same. She tilted her head, question in her eyes. "What is that expression?"

"Certainty," he declared, and leaned forward to kiss her. "Perhaps for the first time in my entire life. What we are going to do about Peter is go to London and get him."

"Get him?" Her eyes went wide. Wide and joyful and he knew that this was exactly what she desired, as well.

He nodded. "He is ours, isn't he? Ours."

She lifted a hand to her lips. "Yes," she said on a broken gasp. "Yes, he is ours. Is that truly how you feel?"

"It is," he admitted. "I don't think any of us will be truly complete without each other. So what we will do, my dear, is follow that man to London and not give up until he agrees to our terms."

She wrapped her arms around him with a girlish squeal and hugged him so tight that he almost couldn't breathe. "This is my favorite birthday," she whispered.

He leaned back and smiled at her, then slowly lowered her back on the settee. "I agree. It will only be better when we win him."

She let out a long sigh and drew his mouth to hers. "Tomorrow," she murmured.

"Tomorrow," he agreed, and covered her again, completely certain of this decision. He only hoped that together, he and Merritt could make Peter feel the same way.

CHAPTER 14

Peter

Peter had only been back in London for thirty-six hours, but he was already waist-deep in duties for his next play, which was to open in only a fortnight. Normally, he would have been lost in the minutia of every detail, but this time…

Well, this time he felt like he was only going through the motions as he addressed set decisions and listened to the chosen actors rehearse the lines he had so carefully crafted.

It had gotten so bad that he'd finally just excused himself and gone back to his townhouse. Now he swung off his horse, handing over the reins to his man, and started up the stairs.

His butler, Ford, met him at the door. "Good afternoon, Mr. Reid. We weren't expecting you so early."

Peter shook his head. He wasn't about to tell Ford that the reason he wasn't at the theatre was because his mind kept turning on the Marquess and Marchioness of Egerton. That would be a little too honest.

"Not feeling myself, I fear," he said. "I think I might have a lie down and then head back in a few hours." Peter started toward the stairs.

"Yes, sir." Ford shut the door. "I do need to inform you that you have visitors. I told them that you might not return until late, but they insisted on staying until you were back."

Peter froze on the first step and turned back, staring at the servant. "Visitors," he repeated softly. He knew who these visitors were. "Lord and Lady Egerton?"

Ford blinked, as if surprised that he could guess with such specificity. "Er, yes, sir. That is correct."

Peter's hands began to shake and he smoothed them along the front of his trousers gently. "I will see them," he said softly. "In fact, if you'd like to take the afternoon off with pay, you and the rest of the staff, I would like to offer that."

Ford's eyes went wide. "I...of course, sir. I will tell Franny and Nan, as well as Buckley and Winston. I'm sure they will be very pleased."

"Good," Peter said, and smiled as Ford inclined his head and hurried off to tell the kitchen staff, maid, footman and driver. They would all scatter within half an hour, he assumed. Enough time to have this encounter, and then...

Well, he couldn't imagine then what. It all depended upon what Elliot and Merry had come here to say. It would be life altering, though. He only knew that for certain.

He moved to the parlor door and drew a few long breaths before he opened it and stepped inside.

Merry and Elliot were seated together on his settee and they both jumped to their feet as he entered. For a moment there was only silence between them all as they all stared like they'd been parted for months, not days. Peter's hand shook as he reached back and shut the door. Locked the door.

He didn't want interruptions, whether the two had come for better or for worse.

"I feel like I have imagined you two in my home for so long, I almost cannot tell if this is real," he said at last.

Merry smiled slightly, her nervousness clear. "It is very real," she assured him.

Peter let his gaze slide to Elliot. The marquess was, of course, much harder to read than his wife. That habit had not died, no matter what had happened since Peter's departure from the cottage.

"May I get you something to drink?" Peter asked, motioning to the fully stocked sideboard. "I've excused the servants, but I'm capable of making tea if you'd prefer."

Elliot made a low grumble in his throat and then came across the room in a few long strides. "We didn't come here for bloody tea," he snapped before he caught Peter around the waist and drew him up against him, crushing his mouth down on his in desperation.

Peter let out a long moan as he wrapped his arms around Elliot's neck and returned the kiss, reveling in this man's taste. In the command that he wielded…except in those lovely moments where he handed it over to Peter.

At last, they pulled away from each other, and Elliot leaned back and motioned to Merry to join them. "Kiss your love, my love."

She smiled, and in that wide and bright expression Peter saw her joy. She all but skipped to him and bounded against both men, kissing first Peter long and deep and then turning toward Elliot. "I will kiss both my loves, thank you very much, my lord."

She then kissed him, and Elliot's low chuckle against her mouth sent a cascade of desire through Peter that almost buckled his knees.

"Now come," she said when she parted from Elliot. She took each of their hands and drew them back to the settee. "We have much to discuss before we do the thing I can see we all wish to do."

"Yes, we do have much to discuss, it seems," Peter said as Merry sat. Elliot took a place on one side of her and Peter on the other, but the marquess reached across the back of the settee to entwine his fingers with Peter's. That simple act sent a shudder through him that seemed to shatter his very soul.

"I will begin," Merry said, and glanced at Elliot.

He nodded. "My wife has a better way with words. *She* will begin."

She smiled. "The way we left things at the cottage was not acceptable," she said. "But I suppose it was necessary."

"I assume this means you two…talked…about what you saw that last day, Elliot?" Peter asked.

Elliot shifted slightly. "Yes. But the truth of the matter is that I didn't need to talk about what I saw. I love that you and Merritt are passionate together. It arouses me beyond measure to watch you two learn each other's bodies. To find new ways to pleasure her from watching your hands move over her skin. That was *never* the issue. And the issue wasn't with the fact that you two loved each other, either. I realize that now."

Peter wrinkled his brow in confusion. "Then what is the issue, exactly?"

"That I…" He looked at Merry and she nodded in encouragement before she took his free hand. It seemed to buoy him up. "God, I'm terrible at this. Couldn't I just fill a bath for you?"

Peter couldn't help but laugh, and Merry did the same. "Afterward, I'm sure that would be lovely, dear," she said. "Now go on."

Elliot huffed out a sigh. "The issue is that I am in love with my wife." He drew in a long breath. "And I am…falling in love…with you."

Peter blinked, staring at this remarkable man who always seemed to certain and yet in this moment was vulnerable and unsure as he struggled to hold Peter's gaze.

"I…have been for some time," Elliot admitted very softly. "But you know that admitting that sort of feeling is difficult for me. And even more difficult since I didn't know if those feelings would be returned by either of you. Seeing how easy it was for you two to love each other, made me feel I had no place in your bond."

"But Elliot knows now that I love him," Merry said before she turned toward him and reached up to touch his cheek.

The marquess's reaction, the way his gaze softened with joy and relief, nearly brought tears to Peter's eyes. It was poetry to see it. It was what bards like him tried to capture in an entire play, and yet there it was in one beautiful man's soft smile.

"I don't expect you to love me," Elliot explained. "You don't know me very well. But it is clear to me now that if I don't…say it…then I might very well lose what I hold the most dear. And I cannot do that, Peter. I can't lose you. Or Merritt. I can't watch you two lose each other and have any hope for my own happiness."

Peter drew back, almost too shocked to speak as the words flowed over him. "You…can't lose us and you don't want us to lose each other," he repeated. "What…what does that mean?"

"We've talked about it a great deal," Merry said. "All the way home from Brighton and in all the hours before we left. Peter, we want all of us to be together. The three of us. If that is something you want."

Peter stared at her, this woman he had loved and lost and never believed he could have again. But she was offering a future with her. And more than that, a future with Elliot. He shifted his gaze to the marquess and shivered at the focused power of what he returned.

Of the feelings that burned in Peter's chest when he thought of loving him. Of loving her. Of loving them. And of being loved in all those same permutations.

"Is it what you want?" Elliot asked.

Peter knew he wasn't just asking about the idea of the three of them together. He leaned in, over Merry. Elliot met him halfway, shivered when Peter cupped his cheek.

"I do love you," he admitted. "I have been falling in love you, almost against my will, for some time, Elliot."

Merry let out a happy, tearful gasp. "Then what is stopping us from doing this? From loving each other like we did at the cottage? From becoming so much more as three than we are as one or two?"

"Societal expectation?" Peter said with a laugh.

Elliot snorted. "Please. I've been your patron for years. Artists are often close with those who finance them. They travel with them, they even live with them. What would be different?"

"Your servants wouldn't talk?" Peter asked.

Merry shook her head. "They haven't talked about anything else they've seen or heard. For all the world knows, we are a very staid couple. Powerful, yes, but passionate? And if the servants wished the world to know the truth, it would be out there, I assure you."

Peter bent his head. "This is almost too good to believe. Could we be so happy? Could we do something so shocking and right?"

"We could," Elliot said. "And we will, if you agree."

Peter shut his eyes. A lifetime of pleasure had led him to this. Back to the beginning with Merry. No, not the beginning. A new beginning. And the love he felt for both these marvelous people swelled in him as he opened his eyes and said, "Yes."

Elliot grabbed for his shirt, fisting it as he pulled Peter in for a kiss. Merry leaned in and joined it, their tongues all twisting around each other, hands clasping each other, first in joy and then in…more.

Peter pulled away. "Come up to my bed," he said to them both. "And let us seal this very happy agreement, shall we?"

Elliot

Peter's room was very fine, not that it mattered. Elliot stepped into the chamber and all he cared about was if it had a bed big enough for all of them. It did, and he moved to it, stripping out of his jacket and waistcoat before he turned.

He found that Peter had shut the door and now leaned Merritt against it as he kissed her with complete and utter abandon. Elliot shivered at the passion of it, knowing it would soon be shifted to him. Ready for it and for Merritt to get all the pleasure she so richly deserved.

He had never felt such certainty as he did in that moment, never felt such warmth and acceptance that existed through this love for both of them. It was like coming home.

And when he revealed his final secret, when he asked for the last step along this path to be complete, then he, too, would be complete.

He moved toward Peter and Merritt, and as he reached them, Merritt stepped away from one lover and into his arms. She lifted her lips to him, red from kissing, and he claimed them, losing himself in her flavor. Peter moved behind her, unfastening her gown as she lifted against Elliot with a long, deep moan of pleasure.

Elliot helped Peter remove the gown and the chemise beneath. Together they went down on their knees before her. Their hands intertwined against her thighs as they each began to lick her. Elliot at her front, flicking her clitoris with the tip of his tongue, Peter behind her, stroking her sex and the tightness of her bottom.

She ground between them, her fingers digging into both their hair as she gasped and sighed out her pleasure. Elliot pushed at her legs and she widened them, allowing each man to slide a finger inside her. She threw her head back, her sheath rippling as they moved in tandem, stroking and stroking, rubbing the rough patch of flesh deep within her that made her shake.

She came in a heady burst of flavor against Elliot's tongue and he couldn't help but moan against her as he lapped it all up. She went limp against them and Elliot stood, sweeping her up and depositing her on the bed where she spread out, touching herself as the two men turned to each other.

Elliot licked his lips, still salty-sweet from her release. Peter Reid looked good enough to eat. Which, he supposed, was almost the ultimate goal. Almost.

He moved toward him, pushing his jacket away, going to work on his cravat as Peter unbuttoned his shirt. Together they pulled the fabric from his waistband. As Peter tugged the shirt over his head, Elliot rubbed his hands along his torso, memorizing the ridges of muscle there and the way Peter sharply inhaled when Elliot's nails raked gently against his flesh.

"My God, I could just touch you for hours," Elliot admitted, leaning in to lick the spot where Peter's shoulder met his neck. "Lie between you and just touch you both."

"Mmm, as lovely as that sounds," Peter said, his voice rough and shaking, "I think I'd like it if you did more than just touch me. Would you like to have me, my lord?"

Elliot slowed the glide of his hands against Peter's skin. "No," he said.

Peter's brow wrinkled. "Well, that is unexpected," he said on a nervous laugh.

"Not because I don't want to feel my cock in you," Elliot said with a moan at the idea. "Oh, I very much do. But today...I want you to fuck me."

He glanced at Merritt and found she was leaning forward, watching the exchange, hardly breathing from the sexual excitement on her face.

Peter swallowed hard. "Are...are you ready for that?"

"He is," Merritt said softly. "We kept up the training, the entire time we were apart. And I promise you, the marquess is very ready. And I'm ready to watch my husband shake with pleasure as you take him."

Both Elliot and Peter shuddered at the needy sound of her voice. At the way her nipples puckered and her slick sex shivered like she was already ready to come again.

Peter moved to her and dug his fingers into her hair, pulling her in for a kiss. When he parted from her, he glanced back at Elliot. "Take your clothes off." He looked down at Merritt. "Suck me."

She moaned as she shifted to her knees and then onto her stomach. Elliot stared as Peter shrugged from his trousers. He had hardly gotten them off when Merritt took him all the way to the back of her throat. She looked at Elliot as she did it, wetting the man who would fuck him.

He felt hard as steel as he undressed. Distracted by the intensely erotic vision of Peter fucking his wife's mouth as she drooled around him, making him wet for what was about to come. At last Elliot was naked and he moved toward them. He stood beside Peter, and Merritt's eyes lit up. She caught his cock in her hand, stroking him as she kept sucking Peter. Then she switched, swirling her tongue around the desperately sensitive head of his cock and taking him deep as she fisted Peter.

"Fucking hell," Elliot said in a garbled tone.

Peter laughed, but the sound was just as strained. "Indeed."

Merritt continued like that for a while, sucking one of them, then the other, moaning as she did it, humping at the bed to find some echo of pleasure. At last Peter stepped away from her. She focused entirely on Elliot now, watching him as she slowed her mouth, tormenting him just as he liked it. He heard Peter getting things from the drawer and then he was at Elliot's back.

"Merritt," he said, his tone sharp.

She withdrew her mouth with a pout. "Yes?"

"Lie on your back and open your legs for him," Peter said softly. "Bend over her, Elliot. No touching, not yet. I want you to feel every stretch of me."

Elliot grunted but did as he was told, leaning over Merritt and lifting his arse for Peter. When he did so, he heard the other man's gasp and smiled. He had discovered the toy, embedded deep so he was already stretched.

"My two wicked angels," Peter said as he fingered the flat end of the plug. "Giving me such lovely gifts. I suppose I should return the favor."

As he said it, he began to remove the plug. The release of the tension made Elliot tremble and he pressed a fist into the mattress on either side of Merry's head. She lifted, drawing her lips across his jawline.

"Isn't it such gorgeous torture?" she whispered. "God, doesn't it make you want to come even before he's taken you?"

Elliot looked down at her and nodded. He held her gaze, finding purchase there as Peter set the toy aside and began to finger him with a digit wet with oil. The pleasure was deep and wicked, pulsing through him and making him push back to get more.

"So greedy," Peter murmured, and pushed his hips against Elliot. He rubbed the head of his cock against Elliot's balls and he hissed out even more pleasure. "Now tell me to put it in you."

"Please!" Elliot gasped. "Do it."

Peter didn't ask again, he didn't tease anymore. He positioned himself and slowly eased forward, stretching Elliot further than he'd ever been stretched, sending that edge of pleasure and pain through every part of him. Making his own cock twitch with desire to bury it inside Merry. Inside Peter. He just wanted to come.

Peter leaned over him as he entered the final few inches. He held still, letting Elliot get used to the feel of being stretched and filled, and then he thrust. Once, twice. Elliot gripped the sheets, nearly rending them in two at the sensation. God, it was better than he'd ever secretly dreamed. A full surrender and yet he felt he'd lost nothing.

Only gained it all.

"Take her," Peter said softly. "Touch him."

They both followed their orders. Merritt grasped Elliot's cock, stroking him as he aligned himself to her. He slid inside with no resistance, she was so wet, and nearly spent right then and there.

She nodded. "It's all for you, love. Just take it. Take it all."

That permission given, Elliot began to fuck her, hard and fast. She stroked herself in time, watching him with wide eyes as he was thrust between them. Back and forth from one pleasure to another. The two sensations so delicious that he could barely stand it. He felt the edge of release there. He couldn't deny it, not this time, not the first time. He grunted in helpless pleasure as he came, pouring into Merritt as her fingers increased against her clitoris. He felt her begin to come as he faded and reveled in the flex of her.

Behind him, Peter had begun to pant, his hands pressing hard into Elliot's shoulders. He said Elliot's name, possessive and hot, loving and owning, and then the heat of him rippled inside Elliot.

He collapsed on the bed over Merry and she captured his mouth, kissing him as Peter lay down beside them and did the same.

He relaxed against them both, feeling them care for him with gentle hands and lips. Loving how they reached for each other alongside him.

And knowing this would be the way it was for the rest of their lives. A future where none of them had to lose, where all of them could love each other.

And it was so beautiful that as he gathered them both close, he felt the sting of tears behind his eyes. And he surrendered to that swell of emotion, just as he had found himself able to finally surrender to the two people he loved most.

And would love until the day he drew his last breath.

EPILOGUE

Six months later

Merritt

The thunderous applause of the audience was music to Merritt's ears as she stood in the wings of the theatre next to Elliot, waiting for Peter to return from his third bow. The play he had been producing when they'd first returned to London from the cottage had been a roaring success, making him an even bigger toast of the town. This final night of its production had been standing room only, with the audience waiting on every beautiful word Peter had written.

She saw the joy of that fact on his face as he came down the stairs from the stage toward Merritt and Elliot. After the actors had all passed by, congratulating Peter as they went to their dressing rooms, she embraced him first, feeling the firm warmth of him against her body and wanting so much to celebrate privately with him.

"It was wonderful, my love," she said.

When she released him, Elliot took his turn. But he didn't just hug Peter—he bent him back slightly and kissed him so passionately that Peter staggered a little when he was set on his feet.

"Good Lord," he said with a laugh. "You are going to make this the truly greatest night of my life if you continue that, Elliot."

"That's my intention," Elliot said with a saucy wink at Peter before he cupped Merritt's arse and gave it a squeeze. "Watching your success makes me hungry for you both."

"And that kind of support is exactly why you are so loved," Peter said with a smile. "But before we can retire to the Donville Masquerade and our very much anticipated celebrations there...I must at least make an appearance at the cast party with our illustrious patrons, the Marquess and Marchioness of Egerton. So come along and be a good boy while you wait."

Peter slung an arm around Elliot's shoulders and the two men laughed as they headed down the hallway together with Merritt at their heels. She loved watching them together, their bond so strong. Their passion for each other as powerful as it was for her. Something they all proved on a regular basis.

In truth, she had never been so happy as she had been the past six months. Not just because she was having amazing, toe-curling, life-altering sex with the two most talented lovers in all the world. But because the love the three shared was only growing with each day.

Tears flooded her eyes as she thought of it. Thought of how she had lost one man and nearly lost the other...but in the end, they had all ended up so very happy.

How in the end, she was well and truly their marchioness. And she always would be.

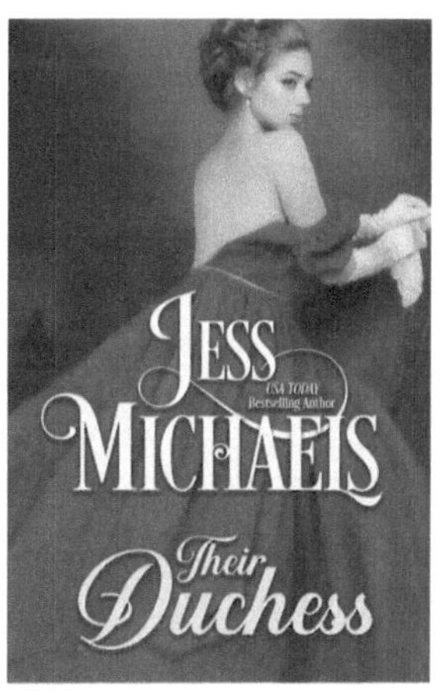

Order Now!

Oliver Wynn gripped the reins tighter and knew it wouldn't help at all. He'd been a driver long enough to know when a situation was hopeless. They weren't going to make it. The rain had turned to ice, the roads were slick and treacherous and the cold was biting. Even through his thick gloves, his fingers felt frozen.

He could only imagine the Duchess of Sedgewick, his longtime employer, was little more comfortable in the carriage he drove. And if he didn't get them to someplace safe, her comfort would not be the problem. Her safety would be.

He squinted into the slashing rain and blinked against the weather. There in the distance were…lights. At least he thought they were lights. Perhaps it was just wishful thinking. But it was better than nothing, so he steered the exhausted horses in the direction of the faintest hope. It took longer than he wished. The mud was thick and icy, the animals could only go so fast, but at last they turned through a gate and up a winding drive toward a large manor house on a hill. Oliver could have wept with relief as he pulled the horses up and stretched his fingers. After gripping the reins so tightly in the last few hours of the journey, he could scarcely feel the digits.

He began to maneuver down from the top of the vehicle, being careful on the icy step, just as servants rushed toward the rig.

"Bad weather," one of them grunted as they took the reins of the horses.

"Nearly deadly," Oliver agreed. "I was relieved to see the house. Is your master at home?"

The stablehand nodded. "Oh yes. Mr. Pembroke is in residence. And I'm certain he will put your passengers up." The young man glanced over his shoulder toward the house. "There he is now. You may speak to him, yourself."

Oliver smoothed his sodden coat and moved toward the steps and the man who stood at the top of them. As he neared him, his breath caught. The master of this house was very handsome, indeed, with lightly graying dark blond hair and eyes so brightly blue that they were impossible not to look at. He had a strong jaw and full lips. It was an intelligent face. A commanding face.

He was casually dressed, with no jacket or cravat, likely because he wasn't expecting company in the middle of an ice storm. His sleeves were rolled to the elbow, and Oliver marked a slash of what appeared to be paint on one of the man's rippled forearms.

He shook off his reaction to the man and executed a polite nod.

"I beg your pardon, my lord. The Duchess of Sedgewick is my passenger, and as you can see, we were surprised by the weather. I wonder if she might take refuge at your home for the night?"

The man in the doorway's gaze fluttered over Oliver in a slow, heavy glance that made every muscle in Oliver's body tighten with tension. Not unpleasant tension, more like awareness. Then he inclined his head.

"Of course," he said. "I would never allow Her Grace…or you… to freeze. Please, let my servants tend to your animals and carriage."

Oliver nodded. He was so cold and so tired from fighting the weather for hours, he could hardly think straight. The idea that someone else would take care of his duties was heavenly. "I will fetch Her Grace, then," he said. "Thank you, my lord."

The gentleman shook his head. "Pembroke," he said. "My grandfather is an earl, but I am no one's lord."

Oliver somehow doubted that was true, but he didn't argue and instead turned back toward the carriage. He drew a long breath before he opened the door and peered inside.

The Duchess of Sedgewick…Anna, beautiful Anna…was cuddled beneath a thick blanket in the corner of the rig. She looked at him with concern.

"Oh, Oliver," she said. "You look cold as ice."

"I'm fine," he lied. "Only sorry that my poor planning put us in such a situation. But we've arrived at the home of a Mr. Pembroke and the gentleman is willing to allow us to stop here for the night."

She shifted and he could see she was uncomfortable. Of course she would be. The man at the door was a stranger, for one. And the trip Anna was making was difficult as it was. Drawing it out likely only made it more so.

But she didn't say any of that. Instead she leaned forward and touched Oliver's gloved hand with her own. Thick layers of fabric separated them, but he still had to fight not to respond to that touch. "You did so very well. Thank you for taking care of me and getting me here safely."

He swallowed past a suddenly thick throat before he croaked out, "Come. Let me escort you over the ice to the house."

She nodded, though her blue eyes never left his. Her hand took his more firmly and she leaned on him as she carefully exited the carriage. The softness of her against his body put him on edge, despite the tenuousness of the situation. But then, he'd always been susceptible to all the ways she made him feel. He couldn't control that, even if he controlled everything else.

He got her to the top of the steps at last and she looked up toward their savior. Mr. Pembroke stared down at her, his piercing blue stare sweeping over her from the crown of her head to the tips of her boots and there was a moment where awareness crackled between them. Anna straightened up a little, tilting her head to examine at him more carefully.

And Oliver was both enthralled by the instant attraction that so clearly bound them as well as jealous. Jealous that she wanted this man, that he wanted her in return. That if they chose, they could be free to do something about it. And all Oliver had were memories.

"Mr..." she began.

"Pembroke, Your Grace," he said. "Ezra Pembroke."

"Pembroke," she repeated softly. "Why does that seem so familiar?"

"My grandfather is the Earl of Barrowfield," Pembroke said. "I assume we shared a ballroom or two before I left good Society several years ago."

She nodded. "Yes, I do recognize the earl's name." Oliver heard the slight tension in her voice. "Well, I do appreciate your kindness, Mr. Pembroke."

"Please come in out of the cold, both of you. My servants are already taking your things inside and will tend to the horses as you settle in." He stepped aside and let Anna pass, then Oliver. Oliver couldn't help but note how Pembroke's gaze followed her with obvious interest.

His jaw tightened. The last thing he wanted was to leave Anna with a man who was no better than the one she was heading to see in the first place.

"You must be exhausted after your long day," Pembroke said. "Shall I show you to your chamber first so you may have a moment to yourself before supper?"

Anna glanced back at Oliver, her dark eyes snagging his and holding there. She seemed nervous. Not afraid, but uncertain. He moved forward. "Would you like me to join you, Your Grace? To help you settle anything?"

She nodded. "Yes, Oliver, that would be appreciated."

Order Now!

ALSO BY JESS MICHAELS

Theirs

Their Marchioness

Their Duchess

Their Countess

Regency Royals

To Protect a Princess

Earl's Choice

Princes are Wild

To Kiss a King

The Queen's Man

The Three Mrs

The Unexpected Wife

The Defiant Wife

The Duke's Wife

The Duke's By-Blows

The Love of a Libertine

The Heart of a Hellion

The Matter of a Marquess

The Redemption of a Rogue

The 1797 Club

The Daring Duke

Her Favorite Duke

The Broken Duke

The Silent Duke

The Duke of Nothing

The Undercover Duke

The Duke of Hearts

The Duke Who Lied

The Duke of Desire

The Last Duke

The Scandal Sheet

The Return of Lady Jane

Stealing the Duke

Lady No Says Yes

My Fair Viscount

Guarding the Countess

The House of Pleasure

Seasons

An Affair in Winter

A Spring Deception

One Summer of Surrender

Adored in Autumn

The Wicked Woodleys

Forbidden

Deceived

Tempted

Ruined

Seduced

Fascinated

To see a complete listing of Jess Michaels' titles, please visit:

http://www.authorjessmichaels.com/books

ABOUT THE AUTHOR

USA Today Bestselling author Jess Michaels likes geeky stuff, Vanilla Coke Zero, anything coconut, cheese and her dog, Elton. She is lucky enough to be married to her favorite person in the world and lives in Oregon settled between the ocean and the mountains.

When she's not obsessively checking her steps on Fitbit or trying out new flavors of Greek yogurt, she writes historical romances with smoking hot characters and emotional stories. She has written for numerous publishers and is now fully indie and loving every moment of it (well, almost every moment).

Jess loves to hear from fans! So please feel free to contact her at Jess@AuthorJessMichaels.com.

Jess Michaels offers a free book to members of her newsletter, so sign up on her website:
http://www.AuthorJessMichaels.com/

 facebook.com/JessMichaelsBks

 instagram.com/JessMichaelsBks

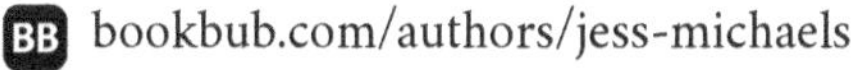 bookbub.com/authors/jess-michaels